To Kate

The Janus Effect

Best Wishes from

Alex

Worldcon '05

The Janus Effect

Alan Cash

This book is gratefully dedicated to all the members of the Birmingham Science Fiction Writers' Group, past and present, for their generous help and criticism over many years.

*Alan Cash,
August 2004*

© Alan Cash & Y Lolfa Cyf., 2005
First impression: 2005

The right of Alan Cash to be identified as author of this work has been asserted by him in accordance with sections 77 and 78 of the Copyright, Designs and Patents Act, 1988.

This book is a work of fiction. Names, characters, places and incidents are either the product of the author's imagination or are used fictitiously.

Cover: Valerie Just

ISBN: 0 86243 769 5

y Lolfa

Printed and published in Wales
by Y Lolfa Cyf., Talybont, Ceredigion SY24 5AP
e-mail ylolfa@ylolfa.com
website www.ylolfa.com
tel. (01970) 832 304
fax 832 782

Contents

	Prologue	6
1	Messages from the Past	7
2	The Time Jacket	39
3	Veema	58
4	Entrapment	70
5	The Gift of Tongues	86
6	The Worms Turn	97
7	Gestalt	110
8	Birmingham 1950	123
9	Birmingham 2010	129
10	Life Streams	141
11	Into the Time Tunnels	155
12	Agent Emerald	166
13	Roentgen	198
14	Eye of the Storm	216
15	The Storm Breaks	226
16	Rendezvous	236

PROLOGUE

The following extracts are taken from Percival's *History of the 21st Century* (Vision Press 3012) and are reproduced here by kind permission of the authors:-

By the middle of the century, the island of Britain was no longer part of a greater Europe, which had, by then, stretched as far as China.

Progressively economically unstable, the British Government looked to harsher and harsher measures to control its population. The Eugenics teachings of John Blenkinsop had eventually led his disciples to force through the passing of The Ancestor (Miscellaneous Provisions) Act 2050, commonly known as The Blenkinsop Law, or The Stunt Law, whereby all those who had any trace of aberration in their family, whether physical or mental, were forbidden to have children. This led to increasing unrest... The origins of John Blenkinsop have been deliberately obfuscated by his acolytes, and records relating to his birth have been destroyed. However, it is believed that he sprang from humble parentage, in the East End of London... One man in particular set out to defy this Law. His origins are equally obscure. His name was Loratu...

– 1 –

Messages from the Past

She was the most beautiful woman that he had ever seen. He had always been attracted to small, slim, dark girls. She fitted this description perfectly.

Moss had answered the door to the safe house, after checking through the spy-hole in the reinforced steel. A young woman stood on the threshold. He could hear her breathing rapidly, when she spoke to him via the entry-phone. He flicked on the porch light just long enough for him to study her face.

"Are you the man they call Loratu?" she asked nervously. "If you are, can I come in? I'm in danger."

Moss pressed the door-release button and she squeezed through the gap before the door was properly open. He hurriedly closed the door behind her. Berbek's troops were liable to come along the road at any moment.

"Who wants to know?"

"I've heard that Loratu recruits for The Cause."

Moss studied her closely. Thick, black curls framed a typically Celtic-type face, from which a pair of tired brown eyes regarded him anxiously. She gave Moss the impression that she had dressed in a hurry. Her mauve trouser suit was splashed with mud, and she carried a small suitcase. The x-ray scanner in the porch showed that she was not carrying a bomb, or a weapon of any description. These days, Moss couldn't afford to take chances.

"If you're thinking of joining us, what do you have to offer?"

"I've just escaped from the Sterilisers," she said.

"That's not much of a recommendation."

"I don't know about that. What I do know is: If I don't sit down soon, I'm going to fall down."

A door opened behind them, and a tall woman in black trousers and sleeveless T-shirt came into the hall. Her hair was cut as if her hairdresser had placed a shallow basin on her head and cut round it. She stared curiously at the new arrival.

"And you are…?"

"My name is Veema Price," the young woman answered quietly.

"I see. Well, Veema, if you were thinking of joining us, let me tell you this: we don't take just anyone. Before we discuss that, however, you must tell me how you found us."

Her grey-green eyes regarded the young woman intently. Veema was too tired to answer. She slumped to the ground and closed her eyes.

"Useless," said the tall woman. "I'll get someone to take her out and lose her." She turned on her heel.

Moss was watching her depart, when he came to a decision. "Just a moment," he called. "Before you do anything like that, we need to find out more about her. She may have told someone where she was going. It could get awkward."

"Very well. On your own head be it."

Moss helped the woman to her feet and led her to a sparsely-furnished sitting room. There was an unshaded light suspended from the ceiling, and beneath it was a small, tatty sofa, with a table alongside. The woman subsided thankfully onto the sofa and Moss thought how small and helpless she looked. A more unlikely recruit he could hardly imagine.

"I suppose you do realise that General Berbek calls us terrorists and would like to eliminate us. You haven't yet told me why you came here. If you think you have any skills to offer us, what are they?"

"I have a degree in psychology from East London University."

Moss laughed and said, "I'm sure that will be useful when you're facing a man charging at you with an assault rifle in his hand. The point is: my colleague had a valid point when she asked how you knew about us and where to find us. You could easily have placed us all in danger by coming here."

"It's simply explained. I noticed someone when I was watching a newsreel report about street violence, and he made an impression on me. I saw the same man again today when I was on the run from the Sterilisers, knew he was one of the Underground terrorists, and followed him. He led me to your door. I stood across the street, trying to work up courage to ring the bell. I have come to offer you my services, if there is any way you can use them."

Moss cursed under his breath, "He's a careless bastard."

From the street, Moss heard the familiar sound of heavy armament. The tall woman burst into the room. Ignoring Veema Price, she said, "They've found us. We've got to get out of here, quick."

Moss reacted by grabbing Veema by the hand and hauling her to her feet.

"You're coming, too," he said, and dragged her towards the door.

"Are you mad? Leave her here. She'll only slow us

down."

"Do you expect me to leave her here to be tortured?" Moss asked.

"Yes. Why not? Come on."

"We're going over the roofs. If you can't make it, you're on your own."

She went to grab her suitcase. "Leave it," he said. "No time." He snatched a rifle and rushed to the door.

They ran up three flights of stairs, Veema hard on Moss's heels, and emerged onto a flat roof. The sky overhead was pitch-black. His sixth sense warned him that a surveillance globe was homing in for the kill. Its searchlight blazed down on him. He lifted the laser-guided rifle to his shoulder and aimed back up the beam. He hit the globe's propulsion unit squarely, and it crashed somewhere out of sight.

At this moment, Veema came out onto the roof. Another globe appeared, rising over the edge of the roof. Out of the shadows, a green ray targeted it, and the globe exploded, raining sharp metal fragments down on Moss. One piece caught him on the right shoulder of his body armour. The tall woman shouted from across the roof, "This way."

Moss ran back to Veema, hoisted her onto his shoulder, and followed the tall woman.

In the maze of condemned buildings that had been left to decay after the collapse of the Thames Barrier, they found refuge in a tenement surrounded by water. No heavy armour could penetrate the flooded streets, some of which were several feet deep in water. The safe house had been deliberately chosen because it backed onto this neighbourhood, where the electricity and mains water had been cut off for years. The only people left here were the Stunts. It was a No Go area that would take weeks to search. One could lose a whole army in it.

The tall woman took a torch from her pack, and used it to examine Moss's shoulder.

"You'll live," she said.

"Let me take a look at it," said Veema.

"What would you know about it?" the woman asked.

"I'm a trained nurse. I should have mentioned it before."

"Well," said Moss, with a grin, "you might be of use to us, after all. My shoulder's beginning to stiffen up. Is there anything to see?"

"It's not too bad, but you should see a doctor."

"Oh, fine! Where am I going to find one of those?"

"I can take you to someone I know," she offered.

"Where is he?"

"Bermondsey. It's too far to walk there now. You'd better get some rest first."

"I think we all need some," said the tall woman. She offered her hand to Veema and said coldly, "My name is Camille."

The three of them set off for Bermondsey at daybreak, dodging from house to house, avoiding as much flood water as they were able to. Moss's arm had begun to swell above the elbow, a sure sign that he had a hairline fracture. Soon, he would be unable to use his right hand, which worried him, although he kept his concerns to himself.

Camille asked Veema, "Are you sure you know the way. Have you been through here recently?"

"Not recently, but I knew it when I was a child. We had relatives in this area. I can find my way to Bermondsey all right."

"It's changed. It's Stunt territory now, and you know what

that means, don't you?"

"I know Stunts are social outcasts, forbidden to breed, forced to live apart, but I have never heard anything that would make me afraid of them."

"No," said Moss. "They are harmless enough, but it's odd that we haven't seen a single one so far today."

"If we turn down this lane," Veema said, "it will save us half a mile."

They turned the corner and heard something crash down behind them.

"What was that?" Veema gasped.

"Look behind you," Camille said. "Someone seems to have blocked the lane."

At that moment, another barrier dropped, this one in front of them. Now, they could go neither forward nor back.

Moss readied his rifle, but it was very painful for him to hold it. He doubted whether he would be able to fire it. Camille scanned the windows of the adjacent buildings, her own rifle ready to fire.

A rough male voice asked, "Who goes there?" His voice echoed off the bare walls.

Moss looked up, but he could see nobody.

"Who wants to know?" he shouted.

It was eerily quiet, except for the sound of water dripping from a broken pipe.

"Where do you think you're going?" the man asked.

"We're looking for a doctor," said Veema.

"Who might you be, girlie?" another man asked.

"My name is Veema."

"Well, Veema, I'm king round here. You have to pay if you want to pass through my land."

"I'm sorry, but we have nothing. We had to leave

everything behind when we were attacked, last night."

"Who attacked you?"

"Berbek's men," Moss said.

"I see," said the first speaker. "Where did this happen?"

"Bonham Avenue."

"Hang on a minute. I know who you are, now. I heard about last night, but I thought you'd been caught. You are Loratu, aren't you?"

"Do I know you?" Moss asked.

"You should know me. I'm One-eyed Jack. I haven't seen you for ages."

"Show yourself. Let me have a proper look at you," Moss shouted.

A small, scruffily dressed man appeared behind a broken window. He was wearing an eye-patch. Moss had to search his memory. It had been a long time, but now he remembered the man.

"It was Stepney, wasn't it? In 2046; during the potato riots."

"That's right," said the man.

Moss heard him call out to someone in the room behind him, to raise the booms.

"Come on up. The stairs are on your right. Watch out for the rats."

Later, while they were sharing a meal of boiled pigeon, Moss explained what had happened on the previous night. His shoulder was now in really bad shape.

"Where's the nearest doctor, Jack? My shoulder took a lump of shrapnel when we were making our escape, and it's in need of attention. My arm is swollen – look," Moss said.

Jack thought for a moment before he replied. "He'd have to be someone who sympathises with your cause. Anyone else would shop you to Berbek's men. The only one I can think of lives about a mile away, in Jameson Street. What's his name, Jonesey?" he asked his companion. "I can't just think of it."

"Doctor Ryan."

"Got a bit of paper and a pencil? I could do you a plan of how to find him."

It was early afternoon when they set out. Moss was lagging behind the women. He was unable to match their pace, and he felt giddy. They had to keep waiting for him to catch up. They had left the Stunts' territory behind and were almost at Dr. Ryan's surgery when Moss, passing an open doorway, was grabbed by someone. Before he realised what had happened, he found himself with a stunner pressed against his head.

"I know you, my friend. You'll earn me a pretty penny from the General."

★ ★ ★

Moss cursed the mole who had sold him out to Berbek. Pain became terror as they wheeled him into the operating theatre. Having failed to wring any information out of him, in spite of weeks of questioning, they were now about to try an experiment. They said it could mean that he would lose at least part of his memory permanently. As he succumbed to the anaesthetic, his last thoughts were: What do they care, as long as they obtain the information about my organisation that they want. God knows how many buried memories might surface, or might vanish for ever. Goodbye, beautiful Veema, I will always love you…

★ ★ ★

Preston, General Berbek's Chief Scientist, looked over to Ackroyd, his sidekick, and asked, "Have you brought the results of today's experiments on Moss, or should we call him Loratu?"

"Yes, I've got them here. Let's have look, shall we? I'll just load them into the viewer."

"How far back did we go into his memory this time round, Ackroyd?"

"We think we took him back as far as 2030. Let's see what we've got. Don't forget, whatever we see now, it is what Moss was looking at, and we could be in for a few surprises."

★ ★ ★

Moss glanced at the computer screen that was set at an angle in the grey metal of the desktop. The appointment diary was flashing. In red, it announced the first visitor of the day: "12/10/2030 – Mr Jonquil (Engov. Security)." The door to the office slid open and the man he was expecting came in. Moss got up from behind his desk and nodded peremptorily.

"Good to see you at last, Mr. Moss," the man said, removing his sunglasses. Jonquil's grey eyes regarded Moss steadily.

"Likewise, Mr. Jonquil. Good trip?"

"Not particularly." Jonquil sat down, folding his tall, spare frame into the chair, without waiting to be asked. Barely a crease showed in his grey, collarless suit. "Guess I don't like space trips. Those shuttles from Cape Canaveral don't get any more comfortable, do they?"

"No. They won't spend the money. Drink?"

"Thanks."

Moss opened a drawer and produced two crystal glasses and an oddly-shaped green bottle.

Jonquil smiled slightly. "They weren't wrong, the guys who described you to me."

"Meaning?"

"You're a fixer. You get things done."

Moss grimaced. "I'd prefer to call myself an enabler." He poured two measures of the golden liquid from the green bottle.

"And that watch I saw on your wrist as you stretched out your hand, Moss; that's an old Rolex, isn't it?"

"Yes, 'fraid so," said Moss, with a laugh he didn't feel. This man made him uncomfortable. He'd already half guessed why he was here.

"What do you want to see first?"

Jonquil attempted to lean back in the metal mesh of the chair "What do you suggest?"

"There's not much to see. We're a very small outfit, as you know. We only rent a part of Eurocom One from The Combine. You must also know we, too, have trouble with shortage of funds; the government officially denies our existence, so we can hardly put pressure on anyone. We have a very small gymnasium. You'll have to continue your daily weight training; the artificial gravity of this space station doesn't prevent a certain loss of bone mass."

Jonquil leaned forward and helped himself to another drink, savoured it and then said conversationally, "The Stunt riots have been worse lately."

It hasn't taken long for him to show his hand, thought

Moss. He replied pleasantly, "I've heard London gets worse and worse. When the Thames barrier went, last winter, the whole East End was flooded. With the huge population movement of the dispossessed, it was bound to happen."

"You wouldn't have had anything to do with that, would you?"

Moss affected surprise. "Whatever gave you that idea?"

"We've discovered one or two things about you, Moss, that don't add up."

"And what do you think I could do about it, stuck up here on Eurocom One?"

"That remains to be seen, but from now on, someone else will be doing your job."

"Just like that?"

"Just like that. We know you're very good at your work on population control in the southeast, but you are not irreplaceable. I'd be interested to know why Administrator Berbek gave you a job in the first place."

"Perhaps he spotted a bright lad?"

"Maybe, you're a bit too bright," said Jonquil. "Genetic engineering was never going to be a total solution to our population problems. The Natural Birthers will always be with us. There'll always be resentment towards compulsory identity cards, because of the hidden information they carry. These natural childbirth maniacs will always refuse to carry their cards, or claim to have lost them."

"So?" said Moss.

"The shuttle's returning to Earth in four hours. I suggest you say your goodbyes," said Jonquil. He drained his glass and stood up. "Oh, and you might like to put a call through to Veema. I believe you consider her to be your common-law wife. You won't be seeing her for quite a while. There's no need to tidy up your office. I've brought your replacement with me. I suggest you have your last look at Earth while I go and fetch him."

Jonquil stretched out his hand and pressed a button on the surface of the desk. The protective shutter in the wall slid up. They both looked down on the familiar scene of a changed Earth. It was very different now from what Moss remembered from his childhood picture books. The deserts were bigger. The southern edge of Britain had disappeared into the sea. The east coast was partially submerged. The north was greener, while the south was parched. This view never failed to frighten him.

"That's where you're going," said Jonquil, pointing to the island of Guernsey.

"The Fortress," whispered Moss, ice forming in the pit of his stomach.

"They're waiting for you. Have a nice time." Jonquil left the room.

Moss continued to stare down at Guernsey. He knew what it meant to be imprisoned there. He would never get out.

★ ★ ★

The double doors of the operating theatre closed with a quiet thump behind Dalziel. His superior, Curtis, looked up from the operating table. There was no one else in the room, for reasons of security.

"I'm having a bit of trouble." His voice was slightly muffled behind the green surgical mask.

"Who's the patient?"

"Have you been down a hole or something? You surely know who it is."

"It could be anyone under all those bandages," Dalziel said.

"Yes. They aren't gentle in Interrogation."

"So, who is it?" asked Dalziel, coming forward.

"Loratu."

"The terrorist?"

"What you call him depends on your point of view."

"Surely, you don't think…?"

"We're not paid to think," said Curtis. "We're paid to find out. The sooner you come to terms with that, the better. You are scrubbed up, aren't you?"

"Yes, of course."

"Get some gloves on. I'll just remove the bandages from his head."

After the dressings had come off, Dalziel saw the bruised and cut face of a man in his forties. He had thinning brown hair and several days' growth of stubble. Even with those injuries, he recognised the face that had stared out of a hundred news outlets. Poor bugger, he thought. Nobody deserves this, least of all him.

"What's the trouble, then?" he asked.

Curtis dropped the bandages into a bin. "We tried yesterday to get a picture on this thing." He gestured to the overhead monitor. "It was only partially successful. Trying to get back to the right level in his memory is proving far more difficult than we thought."

"Wasn't it always going to be a problem?" Dalziel said. "This machine is only experimental. I'm surprised it works at all."

Curtis looked up. "The science behind it is sound."

I wish I were far away from here, Dalziel thought. Let someone else butcher this poor man's memories. We are what we remember.

"So, what can I do?" Dalziel asked reluctantly.

"I want you to adjust the electrodes over the scalp when I tell you. There are enough bare patches of skin."

"What happened yesterday?"

"Before the machine went down, we discovered something interesting. We got him back as far as his meeting with Agent Jonquil. Loratu's name, by the way, is really Moss. Did you know that? We are supposed to be trying to discover what started him on the road to being a terrorist."

Dalziel looked up at the monitor screen, which was showing interference patterns. "We'll have to go very carefully; we could block out large parts of his memory."

"Don't tell me my job," said Curtis angrily. "Just reposition the electrodes, when I say. Right, I'm going to turn it on and see what we've got. I want you ready with that intravenous feed. OK. Press the green button now."

The drug flowed silently down into the needle inserted in the man's wrist.

"Any second now," said Curtis.

A grainy picture flickered and wavered onto the monitor hanging from the ceiling, just above eye level, over the operating table. At first, all that could be seen was a dull, backlit red. Then it lifted, like the opening of an eyelid, and a smudge of blue and white gradually became the image of Earth, seen from space. They were inside the patient's head now. He was looking at the Earth through a porthole.

★ ★ ★

Moss turned away from the porthole through which he had been viewing the Earth hanging in space. Where was his office? His stomach lurched, and he realised the nightmare was happening again. Where was he; *when* was he, this time? This thought was suddenly buried under a deluge of other thoughts, and feelings. He was alone again, alone in his tiny bed, in his tiny apartment, on the outer rim of the huge space wheel that was Eurocom One. Welcome back to 2020, he thought grimly.

The apartment computer cleared its throat again, and spoke with a male voice, upper class, but with a hint of deference. It would do for now. Maybe he'd alter it later.

"Liberty, I've been trying to wake you up for the last ten minutes. It's 7.30."

"Bugger! Toast, two slices, and a glass of cold orange juice, and make it snappy, and – er – *don't call me Liberty*!" He hated being called by that awful name with which his mother had saddled him.

"Sorry, Mr. Moss, *sir*" it said, sounding a trifle hurt, if that were possible.

Moss dashed into the bathroom and made a brief attempt to shower, and put on his underpants. Having his head shaved saved him having to wash and dry his hair. He had a perfunctory shave and pulled on his one-piece coverall. While eating, he looked into the computer screen set into the table, to check his diary for that day. He scowled at his reflection in the shiny surface. Did he look bad today, with bags under the eyes; the nose even more beaky than usual; the thin lips pale. Still, she said she'd loved his brown eyes, but their contact had been by video link only, for no women were allowed in Engov's part of the station. How he longed for her touch.

"It's 8 o'clock, Mr. Moss, sir."

"All right, Albert, you can overdo it you know," he

warned the computer. Grabbing his electronic note pad, he punched the door code. "Don't wait up for me, darling."

"Don't you *darling* me, sir!"

"Funny, I always *thought* you were gay!"

The door hissed shut and he was out in the corridor.

The Office of Special Statistics was on the second level. All the living quarters being on the first, he only had to descend one level in the lift. 'Special' meant that Engov didn't want sensitive information to leak out. His Majesty's Government had decided that it was more secure to bury it in a company that was making the next generation of nanotechnology, the ability to create better chips having reached its upper limit. They were paranoid about security.

It was well known that the population of England was fragmenting into the rich, the poor, and the Stunts; the latter were outcasts who wanted nothing to do with controlled births, voluntary euthanasia, or the grip of insurance companies by way of information embedded in identity cards. Voluntary euthanasia? Now there *was* a joke! How did the government dispose of an ageing population? Moss knew. Herd them into old people's homes, and poison their water supplies with mind-altering drugs, so that they became so depressed that anything would be a release.

His work was in 'sensitive' material, which involved population movement and control. Why wasn't it working as well as they wanted it, and how could it be made to work better? He was a small, twenty-year-old cog in a small department, comprising Administrator Berbek and ten underlings. There were no women. They were known to be unreliable. They had to have time off to produce babies. Whether they could, or whether they wanted to return to work after expensive retraining, it was no longer a risk worth taking and it didn't make economic sense to encourage them to come back.

At the lunch interval, he met Atkinson in the small canteen. He was a short, balding, man, whose failure to use a deodorant offended Moss's sensitive nose. After exchanging pleasantries, Atkinson said, "You know we're having difficulty getting our transmissions back to Earth?"

"Yes. Is there anything new on that?"

"They've cracked it. The interference is coming from round Jupiter!"

"Really?" Moss answered, but failed to make eye contact.

"You don't seem very interested."

"Had a bad morning," Moss said, looking down at his vegetable lasagne.

"Not thinking about her again, are you?"

"I think..." Moss was about to say something he would regret. It was never wise to speak too freely, in such a small community. The background musak cut off abruptly and Administrator Berbek's clipped voice came over the P.A.

"Mr. Moss. I would like to see you in my office in five minutes. Thank you."

Atkinson paused in mid mouthful. "What've you been up to?"

"I don't know, but I suspect I'm about to find out."

As he walked down the corridor to Berbek's office, Moss ran over in his mind what could be wrong. Something was always wrong, when Berbek wanted to see him; normally, the Administrator ignored him. He pressed a button on the wall outside Berbek's office, and heard his voice from within.

"Come."

The door slid open and Moss went in.

Administrator Berbek had his back to him; he was watering a spider plant, using a long-spouted jug. Moss stood there for what seemed an age, hardly daring to breathe, his eyes fixed on Berbek's maroon jacket, which was straining its seams over a prodigiously broad back. Finally, Berbek set down the jug, turned, and, with a podgy, coffee-coloured hand, motioned Moss to sit, while he remained standing. Moss sat and looked up at the large man. Berbek's collarless jacket stretched too tightly across his thickening midriff. A thick, bull-like neck supported a round, dark head covered in crinkly, black hair. His eyes were grey and bulged. Moss wondered if the man had a thyroid problem. Berbek smiled, and it was so unusual that Moss didn't know what to make of it.

"You know about the trouble we've been having with the Stunts recently?"

Moss nodded.

"I'll take that as a yes." Then, amazingly, he smiled again. What was he up to? Berbek cleared his throat. "Too many of them are breeding illegally. The only thing that's really holding them in check is that they've no real leader; no one that's any good, that is. However, the moment they find one..." He tailed off.

"As of tomorrow, you'll be joining Atkinson's team. I know you don't like him, but he's got some good men together. I want you to help them to bring the Stunt problem under control. You've come up with some good ideas lately. I want you to go further."

He picked up some papers from his desk and banged them together, edge on, and put them down again carefully. "It'll mean more responsibility and more pay. Don't let me feel I've made a mistake with you, okay? Good morning."

"Good morning, sir."

"Oh, and when you've tidied up your office, you can take the rest of the day off; all right?"

"Thank you, sir."

"Don't thank me, laddie, just use that brain of yours; understood?" Berbek waved his hand dismissively. The interview was over.

Before he knew it, Moss was back in his apartment. Whom should he call first? He phoned his mother. It was expensive to put a call through to Earth, but what the hell! A middle-aged face, lined about the eyes and mouth, and with a bulbous nose, coalesced onto the screen.

"Hi, mum!" he said, trying to sound conversational.

"Yes? What is it? I'm busy." There was a man's voice in the background. She turned away from the screen. "Be quiet, Henry, for a moment! All right, what is it now?"

"Oh, don't be like that, Mum. Listen, I've had a promotion!"

"You had what?"

"There, I knew you'd be proud of me."

"So what've you done? A little arse-licking?"

"Mum!"

"You know you're only up there 'cause you can't get a decent job down here!"

"Oh, thanks, Mum!"

He was about to cut the connection, when she said, "What is your new job, anyway?"

"It's classified," he said smugly, and then he did cut her off.

He was upset that he couldn't get on with his mother. It had always been the same, since his father died. Without his moderating influence, she'd just reverted to what she'd always been. She had never wanted Moss. The fact that he disliked his stepfather didn't help the relationship.

Next, he tried to call Annette. Her image instantly lit up on the small screen, but all her recorded message said was:

"Hello, whoever you are. Sorry, I can't take your call at the moment, but if you'd like to leave your name and number, please speak after the beep."

"Hi! It's me. I just…" He always became tongue-tied when speaking to a machine, though he should be used to it by now. "I'll call you back; got something special to tell you. Bye."

Well, that was all very unsatisfactory. Searching for something to fill the void, he told the computer to turn on the news so that he could watch it on the wallvid screen. It started with an item about the Stunts. More unrest around London. He couldn't really understand that. What did they want from life? Didn't the government provide health care, housing of a sort, food, and jobs, even if he would hate having any of them? He caught sight of a small, dark-haired young girl in the crowd; she was waving a placard with the words NATURAL SELECTION. NATURAL BIRTH, badly painted in red on dog-eared, muddy cardboard. She caught and held Moss's attention. She was extremely attractive and he warmed to her at once. The military were firing gas canisters into the crowd. Then they were wading in, hitting people indiscriminately. Was this what his new job would involve?

The wallvid fizzed, and the picture broke up into a series of multicoloured wavy lines. A sudden chill ran through him as the temperature of the room, normally a constant 18 degrees, plummeted.

"Computer, what's going on?"

It struggled to reply, but the words were slow and mangled. The lights went out. Moss looked round. The air was being sucked out of the room. The bathroom door burst inwards, slamming against the inside wall. There was a black void in there. Running in slow motion towards him was a yellow light in humanoid form. As it drew nearer, it turned into a white figure with a square-topped head. It stretched out a stubby, white hand towards him. He screamed and tried to back away. Oh God, he thought, it's happening again. His buried nightmare spat at him from his childhood.

The automatic sprinkler system exploded into action. Through the hiss of water and steam, the figure stepped into the room, holding a black canister in its hand. At the same time, an unseen force was pulling it remorselessly backwards. With a gesture of despair, the apparition threw the canister on to the carpet. There was a rush of air into the room, and the figure was gone.

Moss collapsed onto the floor, his hands protectively over his head, and lay there, breathing heavily. It was definitely happening again. Was he going mad? Gradually, he calmed down, rolled over onto his back, and pulled in great gasps of air. Something was burning. The light level crept back up. He turned his head. There, half a metre away, was the black canister of his nightmare. Little flames crackled round it, despite the sprinklers, which had died to a trickle. He must extinguish them. He stumbled into the kitchen, filled a jug of water, came back and threw it over the object. It sizzled and the flames went out. He put his hand towards it gingerly but could still feel the heat coming off it. He sat there for what seemed like an age. Eventually, he thought it must be cool enough to touch. He picked it up.

It was warm and heavy. He tried to discover if he could open it. The top came off. Inside was a roll of old papers. He hadn't understood them before, when he was having this same nightmare. He understood them now. The top one in the roll was headed: *Seduction of the Gene Genie*. The full date was unreadable, but the year was 1994. He scanned the page quickly.

'...anything is excusable in the name of law and order. One day, we will have to disclose our own DNA code, at every turn; to get a job, a loan, insurance...'

There was more, but it was badly scorched. He sat there, looking at it and thinking: so, it really had all happened. He was OK, then. Everything was fine, as long as you were law-abiding; so they said. But, what about the people whose DNA profile didn't fit the norm? What did you do with them?

He delicately put down the fragile cutting. Underneath it was a far older one, dated March 3rd, 1953; a copy of an article in a long defunct publication called *Nature,* written by Watson and Crick. He had learned about them when he was in school. The fathers of modern genetics, their work had been harnessed to the pursuit of criminals, rather than to aid people to get better, faster hospital treatment. Nowadays, the thinking was that all men are potential rapists, so their DNA should be on file and accessible to the police.

All the endless information that had been poured into Moss over the years began to fall apart. He realised now that the motive behind modern genetic research was money, big business. It was all about saving money, by breeding better human beings, who didn't get sick so often; and law-abiding citizens, who wouldn't need so much policing. Money was at the bottom of it all; neither care, consideration nor conscience. He wished his father were alive. He was someone who could make sense of all this. There was Uncle Arthur, of course. Perhaps he could help to clarify things.

The room around him grew fuzzy. The next thing he

knew, he was blundering through a wood, looking for something. He burst through the trees and onto a path. A man, who somehow looked strangely familiar, had fallen down and was lying on his back, looking up at him. Moss felt himself being pulled backwards, just as a young woman in a billowing cotton dress came running down the path towards the man. A voice far above him said, "You've bungled it, trying to do it too fast." Moss thought he recognised the voice. Why was it, also, familiar? He realised that he was breathing much too quickly. I must call for help, he thought, I must call for...

He woke up slowly, his mind jumbled; he could remember very little. He just had a feeling of nausea, like waking from a bad dream. There had been something tight round his forehead. A reverberating voice had come from a great distance, shouting, "He's broken out of the net."

"And we still don't know what his motives were!" said someone else.

They don't know? I don't know what they're talking about, Moss thought.

Two eyes had stared down at him from a face half covered by a dark green mask. A hand in a surgical glove, holding a syringe, appeared briefly.

"This will help you to sleep," he heard someone say, and he felt something heavy move up his arm. He had screamed, thrashing about with all his might.

Now, he was on a bed and wearing a hospital gown. A white sheet lay lightly over him. He felt very hot. The whole room was painted light grey. On the wall to his right was a picture. Moss managed to sit up. As he did so, the pearly light in the room grew in brilliance. His head throbbed and he felt sick.

He put out an arm, to steady himself against the bedside

table, and looked in horror as his sleeve slipped back. The skin was bruised, the arm emaciated. With a great effort, he swung his legs over the edge of the bed and planted his feet on the cool floor. Then, he staggered towards the picture. Leaning his open palms on the wall on either side of the picture's frame, he peered at his reflection in the glass. A wild, hollow-eyed face, with an unkempt beard and receding, straggly hair, looked back at him. He saw the face of a man who was not only very ill, but it looked more than twenty years older than he had been, minutes before.

★ ★ ★

Garvie Berbek had made himself very useful at every opportunity. With the military in control of most of southeast England, he made himself a General; he was effectively the real government. The *elected* government had decamped to Birmingham, of all places! Time wasters and ditherers, the lot of them, in his opinion. He smiled and shuddered at the same time. What was needed, and what he intended to give, was 'the smack of firm government'. He remembered the phrase from somewhere. For a start, he'd made himself a general. A dictator? No, of course not. How could anyone think such a thing? The Party of Regeneration had had their chance, and failed. What England needed was someone stronger, and he had great plans for it. Soon, all the country, as far north as Hadrian's Wall, would learn of these plans. The barbarians beyond it deserved his pity, but nothing else. England for the English! He looked at the map of the British Empire on the wall. Pink bits all over the world. Those were the days, and they were going to return.

Meanwhile, there was endless paperwork to plough

through. He thought of abolishing most of it, but the paperless office was, unfortunately, a myth. People wanted something they could hold, feel, screw up and throw in the bin. You couldn't do that with a screen. Electronic books, in his opinion, were an enormous failure. Anyway, reactionary or not, *he* liked the feel of paper between his fingers and thumbs, and to be able to score it deeply with a red pen, when he felt in a bad mood. Where was the pure satisfaction of doing that to a screen? Consigning things to a virtual rubbish bin was no fun at all.

He scanned the next report, and something caught his eye. They were getting nowhere with the interrogation of Loratu, the terrorist, but what was this detail? He prided himself on having a great eye for detail. The report referred him to the attached mini-disk from the medical investigation unit where they were using experimental, mind-probing technology. He put it into the slot in his terminal. The picture was grainy and unsteady, as if seen through the eyes of someone who was running. It was in black and white, which didn't help. A man was sprawled out on a path, his face turned upwards. A young woman, in what looked like a billowing cotton dress, was running towards him through some trees. What was it that was bugging him?

"Freeze frame," he said. The machine obeyed. The man and woman were demonstrably middle-class. "Call up the fashions of the 1990s, for both sexes, and split the screen, leaving the recording on the left."

No. Nothing matched. He asked for the same for the 1980s, 1970s, 1960s and 1950s. With the last, he struck gold. Yes! He had been right. Something had certainly tickled his memory, somehow. Now, why would Loratu be remembering, or dreaming, a scene out of the 1950s? The people on the screen must be related to him in some way. This seemed reasonable. Loratu was now aged 40, so he was born in the year 2000. Berbek drew a file towards him and flicked through the pages. Loratu's parents were aged 36 and 40 at his birth. Arthur Moss, the father, was born in 1964, so, was he looking at Moss's grandparents? How could that be possible?

God knows why Moss called himself Loratu; it had been easy enough to associate him with that *nom de guerre*. Berbek had the full family tree in front of him, and those of Moss's close associates.

That was interesting. He'd never noticed it before. Moss's girlfriend, Veema Price, was also Moss's half cousin. So where did she fit in? He consulted the family tree and called up pictures of Sally Fairin and Robert Llewellyn Moss. There was a very strong similarity between them and the people in the grainy film. They weren't Moss's grandparents. Sally Fairin must have had an affair with Robert Moss and been made pregnant by him. This still left an even more interesting question: why was Moss dreaming of an affair that happened long before he was born? *Could he have actually been there*? No, that was too horrible to contemplate. He couldn't have been, could he?

"Computer, save entire programme and scan these documents."

He removed the relevant pages from Moss's file and fed them into the machine.

"Get me Preston."

"Which Preston, sir?" asked the machine.

Berbek sighed. "Bernard Preston, in Project Alpha."

The logo of a gently flapping Union Jack cleared from the face of another screen, to his right, to show a man of about forty, wearing an olive green uniform, working at some task out of sight. He looked up suddenly and stared at Berbek, who recognised Preston's grey eyes and aquiline nose.

"General Berbek! What an unexpected pleasure!"

"Cut the crap, Bernard. I'm going to transmit some information to you now, so clear a screen. We've got big problems."

★ ★ ★

The ceiling of the huge, decrepit warehouse dripped moisture. The heat of the day had drained away and the night was chilly. That morning there had been a rare downpour of monsoon-like proportions. Pools of stagnant water reflected the dim glare of the city's sky.

Elnac Stavinsky, one-time master safecracker and all-round thief, pulled his grubby coat more tightly around him. He held his small, bony hands out towards the fire. A rusting can hung from a tripod over the flames. In it, rice boiled. It had been fun while it lasted. With all the rich people leaving London, there were fewer things worth stealing. Time, thought Elnac, to be moving on.

He looked across the fire at his companion, a large man in a leather jerkin and stained workman's trousers. The firelight glistened off his bald head. Funny how it all works out, he thought. We should be living in a shiny, metallic city, with our every need catered for. Forty years into the new century, and look at us. Thames Barrier gone. East End flooded. Military bloody everywhere. He sucked in a long breath between uneven teeth.

Bartok dragged a fingerless, dirty glove across his mouth. "Penny for 'em?"

"What? Nar, I was just starin' into the fire, thinkin' things."

"'Ere, You're not gettin' too intro-watsit; not thinkin' too deep, are yer? Never did no one no good, an' that's a fact."

Elnac looked at him and then looked down. "Yer." He poked the fire a bit and listened. The background noise of traffic that had been there all his thirty-six years was stilled. Only the occasional army lorry roared past in the distance. Bartok picked up a sausage, from a pile on grimy paper, and stuck it on the point of a stick. He held it over the fire, and asked, "So, what've you got lined up for us, then?"

If only you knew, thought Elnac. Instead, he said, "I came across somethin' the other day that might be useful."

"What?"

"Somethin' the Ruskies was workin' on."

Bartok drew in a long breath. "Not one of them time-jacket things?"

"Could be. Could be." Elnac leaned forward conspiratorially. There was a pause.

"Yer, well?"

"I reckon this rice is about ready. You done them sausages yet?"

Bartok looked exasperated. "Oh, come on, them time-jacket things is illegal, ain't they?"

"Only 'cause they weren't used right. People was trying to regress back their age with 'em, when they was only s'posed to aid the 'ealing process."

"I wouldn't 'ave nuffin' to do with it, if I was you," said Bartok. "Ain't we in enough trouble already?"

"Comes a time when you ain't bothered no more," said Elnac, settling back on his travelling sack and grinning up at the rusting ceiling supports.

"Yer! In a pig's ear! I know you. How much you give

for it, then?"

"Nothin'," said Elnac. "I stole it!"

"*Stole it*! By the five Saints! You out of your 'ead?"

"Could be."

"I don' believe you. Let's see it, then."

Elnac leaned forward, stopped chewing the plug weed he'd been masticating for the last half hour, and spat it out into the flames. He leaned back again, and thought: that great big lumbering idiot. Still, I've got the brains, and he's got the whatever. Any road, I still need someone to guard my back. God knows what sort of barbarians they are, up north.

"Go on, show us it, then," said Bartok insistently.

"I ain't got it 'ere, yer twit. It's in safekeepin'."

"You let on to someone else about it! That ain't very bright."

This man's getting on my nerves again, Elnac thought. Perhaps I *should* leave him behind. "What was that?' he asked, peering round nervously.

"What you turn roun' for?" Bartok looked jittery.

"Thought I 'eard somethin'"

Bartok was silent for a moment, listening. "Nar. Nobody. I'd 'ave 'eard 'em. Ears like a bat, and I got booby traps all over the place. What do yer want the jacket for, anyway?"

"*I* don't want it," said Elnac, "but *someone* might, *and* we could turn a tidy profit into the bargain."

"Who'd pay for it?"

"Loratu."

"Don't be daft. They got 'im. Dead, or mad, more like. We ain't goin' to see 'im no more," Bartok said, gloomily.

"You think so, do you, O stunt of little brain?"

"Who are you callin' a stunt?" bawled Bartok, levering himself up and bunching his dirty, bitten nails into the palms of his mittens. "I'll 'ave you, you little skinny bag o' bones."

"We're both stunts, you cow 'ead! You know that's why we're outside of the law. We ain't big and strong and blond. We're small and 'airy, an some of us, *some of us,* mind, don't smell so good."

"Yer, like you!" shouted Bartok angrily.

"That's right, tell the world," he said wearily. He thought he saw a movement, and jumped up in alarm. Oh, bloody hell, he thought, it can't be!

"Come out, yer bitch," he yelled.

"Anything you say, little one," a voice whispered in his ear, just as an arm, like an iron rod, tightened under his chin.

"No offence! No offence!" Elnac croaked.

"None taken, I'm sure. Now, show me where this time-jacket is stowed, or we really will be able to see light between your ears."

"No chance!"

The rod-like arm stiffened, bringing Elnac's chin up.

"Do you feel the bones in your neck begin to crack a little? Do you?"

"Yessh."

"Well?"

"No."

"Sure?"

Elnac waved his hand submissively, now that he could no longer speak.

"Good."

Elnac felt the grip relax, to his intense relief, and he slumped to the ground. Slowly, the constriction in his throat cleared enough for him to think. He looked up unsteadily. It really *was* her. Things must be bad. The tall, slim woman, clad in black from neck to toe, looked down on him. Her high cheek-boned, oval face could once have been beautiful, but now looked pinched and drawn. Her black hair was short and cut in a severe line across the top of her ears. Most of all, it was her eyes that held the attention. Sparkling grey-green, they gave not the slightest hint of warmth.

"And don't you make a move, either," she said commandingly to Bartok, who was cautiously trying to crawl away.

Elnac coughed. "What d'you want, anyway?"

"The jacket, cloth ears."

"Well, *I* haven't got it."

"*Well*, let's find it together, shall we?"

"Why should I give it to you?" Elnac asked.

"Because I'm going to give it to Loratu." she said.

"He's alive, then?" Elnac looked disbelieving.

"I believe so, but, the General's got him."

Bartok spat. "Bleedin' Berbek. You'll never do it."

Elnac got up and looked the woman full in the face. "What's in it for us?"

Returning his look, she asked, "Do you want to help me get Loratu back, or not?"

★ ★ ★

Berbek stared agitatedly at the screen. Why hadn't the wretched Preston got back to him? It had been days since their last contact.

"Get me Bernard Preston."

"Right away, sir." The female voice of the computer was obsequious. He'd replaced its last persona, for being too clever. The slowly flapping Union Jack logo gave way to Preston's face; he was in the act of taking off his glasses.

Berbek looked at him sharply. "Well?"

"Most interesting," Preston said.

"Yes, yes, but what does it all *mean*?"

"Your Mr. Moss has got into Project Alpha."

"But how?"

"We're still checking. Some of the records appear to have been tampered with."

"What do you need to complete the project? I need results even faster, now we know that Moss knows about Alpha."

"More time."

"Spare me the irony, Bernard."

"Do your medics know what we've stumbled on?"

"I don't know," said Berbek, "but I've taken Curtis and Dalziel off the case. I think they're due for some *permanent* leave."

Preston looked stunned for a moment. "If that means what I think it means, it would be a very stupid move. They're very experienced surgeons, and we both need them."

"Don't you dare question my decisions," Berbek said angrily. "I can have you removed just as easily."

"And lose your best scientist into the bargain? I think not."

Berbek pursed his lips. Preston was right, damn him; but still, he couldn't risk a security leak.

"Suppose you make both of them an offer they can't refuse," said Preston reasonably.

Berbek smiled. "Or, perhaps, just one of them?"

– 2 –

The Time Jacket

Dalziel was lying on his bed, in the medical complex, reading a collection of detective stories by that extraordinary author, Conan Doyle. They spoke of a world he found very difficult to relate to, with shifting fogs, cold, damp winters, and poor internal heating, where everything was seemingly shrouded in smoke. Nonetheless, they were good stories and he loved a good story, especially a detective story.

He had sent off reports of the day's work to General Berbek, and was taking a well-earned rest. They were delving ever deeper into Loratu's subconscious, and some very strange things were beginning to appear, things that Loratu couldn't possibly have known about, *unless he was actually there*. Everyone knew that time travel was impossible; it was just something dreamt up by that wonderful guy, Herbert Wells, in another of Dalziel's favourite stories.

There was a knock on the door. He glanced at the screen by his bedside. It was just past twenty-one thirty.

"Come in; door's open!"

The panel slid back, to reveal Curtis, holding two glasses and a bottle of red wine, and wearing a rather fake smile,

Dalziel thought. He'd learnt to be rather wary of Curtis. Superiors were never to be trusted, especially this one, who seemed to have the all-consuming zeal of the recently converted to the new state of things. Also, Curtis had never fraternised with him before.

"Thought we might have a drink!" said Curtis, entering the room and putting down his cargo on a low table at the end of the bed.

"In honour of what?" Dalziel asked.

"Of the great work we're doing. The general is very impressed."

"I see. But you know I don't drink."

"Just a little won't hurt, surely?"

"Well, if you insist." He thought it best not to upset the man.

"Oh, I do, I do." Curtis settled himself on the end of the bed, twisted the seal off the top of the bottle, and poured out half a glass each.

Dalziel didn't like drinking alcohol; he liked red wine least of all. "What is it?"

"Nothing but the best! Liebstraumer 1998!"

He'd never heard of it, but that didn't mean anything. Curtis handed him a glass.

"Cheers!"

"Cheers." He took a tentative sip. It was warm on the tongue, with a sharp taste of berries.

"You must get very lonely."

Heavens, the man was getting personal already, Dalziel thought.

"No wife and children, not even a girlfriend, I hear?"

Dalziel took another sip. It wasn't too bad. "I get by."

"So, what do you do in your spare time?"

"I read. I watch three-dimensional opera."

"Really? I hear that opera disks are still quite expensive."

"Well, I haven't got anything else to spend my money on," he said.

"You know, Berbek's quite ruthless," Curtis said confidentially.

"Pardon?"

"You heard what I said."

"And so?"

"He intends to do away with us."

"Why? We're very useful to him."

Curtis put down his glass. "But we're gaining too much knowledge. In the wrong hands, if you get my drift, it could be dangerous for us."

"So, you think there really is something in this time travel idea?" Dalziel took another, larger sip. It really was very good.

"There's been a whisper that the government were researching into this."

"But everyone knows it can't be done."

"Well, perhaps they found a way."

He decided to be very cautious. "Who did you hear all this from?"

"Oh, come on," said Curtis, leaning forward conspiratorially, and smiling even more. "We both know who I mean, don't we?"

Dalziel took another sip. It was the way that the slightly salty tang exploded into warmth on the back of the throat that he enjoyed. It could become addictive. "I'm sorry, Curtis, I don't know who you're talking about."

Curtis's face changed. "Oh, well, if you're going to be

awkward about it, forget I spoke."

Dalziel heard this as from a great distance, and noticed in a detached way, that Curtis looked somehow older, and that his voice was echoing. He was so tired.

★ ★ ★

When Dalziel woke up, he felt very cold. He wasn't on his bed. What's more, it was dark all around him. He heard a heavy vehicle rumble past in the distance. To his left was a long grey wall. Underneath him was something hard and wet that was beginning to soak through his sweatshirt and trousers. There was something bulking out his right trouser pocket. He sat up against the wall, pulled it out and examined it. It was a small stone with a strip of paper wrapped around it. The writing was very thin, spidery and difficult to make out, but there was a full moon almost directly overhead, which enabled him to read it.

This is your only chance to get out. Take it. Curtis.

That was all very well, but how and where was he to go? He'd heard of the People of the Mist. Everyone had. The problem was that they were scattered. Hadn't he just spent the last week probing the memories of their leader, poor sod?

He got up gingerly, and immediately felt something hard in the small of his back.

"Well, this is a surprise. I thought all good boys were tucked up in bed at this time of night," said a quiet female voice. "Put your hands behind your head and turn around very slowly, so that I can see you."

He knew that voice. It had been on a thousand clandestine broadcasts. He didn't move.

"They said you were dead."

"Well, that's another thing they've got wrong, isn't it?"

He couldn't place her accent exactly, but there was a trace of Welsh about it.

"What are you going to do?" Dalziel asked.

"You're an unexpected treasure. You're going to take me to the man who you've been experimenting on."

"Who would that be?"

"This is no time to be coy," she said. "Berbek wants you dead. If you want to live, you've no choice but to help us; it's as simple as that."

"And if I don't?"

"Then you'll die without ever seeing my face," she said.

He was going to have to chance it. Very slowly, he raised his hands until they were clasped behind his head. He turned around and faced a woman, who was barely visible, except for her pale face and grey-green eyes. No wonder they called her The Lady in Black.

"I thought I'd never meet you, except under a scalpel, Camille."

"Don't get personal with me. I'm going to take you to meet some new friends, and then we're going to get Loratu out. Are you going to help us?"

"On one condition."

"Let's hear it."

"I join your organisation."

"We'll see how good you are at this job first," she said, gesturing him to follow, using the glue gun she had been poking into his back.

"And, you're going to do this on your own?"

"No." She spoke inaudibly into something on her wrist. Round the corner of the building came a small, wiry, slightly stooped man, and a taller, broader one, with a bald head. They seemed to be dressed in little more than rags.

"And this is your organisation? Things must be worse than I thought," he said.

"Come on," she said, turning her back on him and looking over her shoulder.

★ ★ ★

Moss was running down a corridor of light. At the end of the corridor was a room that was somehow familiar. In it was a man, a frightened man, backing away. He, too, was familiar to Moss. It dawned on him that the other man was himself, as he would have looked, twenty years earlier. It was raining, not just gentle rain, but a waterfall. With great effort, he threw a canister onto the carpet, and then he was sucked back into the light.

He woke up, shivering. Sweat was running into his eyes. Now that he knew who the man was, and that it was himself, he was sure that he *was* going mad. He tried to call out, but nothing happened, at least, nothing he could hear. The room came back into focus. It was the same as before, with pale grey walls and a picture. A single white sheet was over him. In the corner, he noticed the unblinking eye of a camera. It was bigger and more obvious than he expected. Didn't they have smaller things these days? But then, again, if it works, why change it?

What time was it? What day was it? Moss ached all over. Who am I? I can't remember a thing except being younger. I remember working for a man called Berbek, on a space station called Eurocom One. I was working on statistics, crowd control. I forget. Then, this man came to see me, didn't he? No, that was later, much later. Did it happen at all? I remember my twentieth birthday. After that, my life seems like a void, or worse. There is a blackness that has pain scored through it; little flashes of scenes, like a badly edited film, with blackness in between.

★ ★ ★

His head was a ball of pain, especially behind his left eye and over the left side of his head. He felt that he must have something cool to put over it. He looked towards the side table. Hanging over the rail were a towel and a face flannel. With shaking muscles, he stretched out but failed to reach them. He managed to drag himself into a sitting position, and reaching out again, he pulled the face flannel off the rail. He doused it with some water from a glass that someone had thoughtfully provided, and put it over his aching eye. He lay back. Get a grip now, he told himself. It'll be all right soon.

What was that? Without knowing it, he had lapsed into a doze. The whisper was repeated.

"Don't move. Pretend to be asleep. It's all right. We're going to get you out. First, I shall inject you with something that will make you sleep."

He felt a pinprick somewhere in his right thigh. It didn't take long; soon the pain began to ebb. He was vaguely aware of being moved at speed, with lights flashing overhead, echoing voices, and a revving engine.

"I hope you didn't give him too much." The female voice had a trace of a Welsh accent.

"You let me do my job; you do yours," the man said.

After that, Moss remembered being jostled, and feeling

very sick. The first thing he was truly aware of was light showing through his eyelids. Very slowly, sound increased. He was afraid of opening his eyes; afraid of what he might see.

★ ★ ★

General Berbek looked up as the door-chime sounded. He pressed the entry button and the door slid back. Curtis came in. Berbek glared at him.

"Yes, what is it?"

"I've done what we agreed."

"So, he's dead, then?"

"Yes."

"Very well. Good morning." Berbek waved his hand dismissively.

"So you'll allow me to continue with my work?" Curtis asked.

"Yes, yes. Provided your silence is assured. I had my doubts about you and Dalziel, but I suppose you've proved your worth to the cause. Anyway, now you have a murder hanging over you I can pull you in any time I like, can't I?"

Curtis bowed his head and nodded.

"Right. Dismissed."

Curtis backed out of the room and the door closed. The screen on Berbek's left came to life, insistently beeping. Berbek pressed the keypad in front of it and the face of his security chief, a brown-skinned man with a silvery, short beard, looked up from the screen.

"Yes, what is it, Mehmet?"

The man looked terrified. His lips moved but nothing came out.

"Yes?"

"Loratu's escaped."

"*What?*" In frustration, Berbek slammed his fist down on the desk.

"It all seemed quite OK. Dalziel said he had orders to escort him to another part of the building."

"*Dalziel?*"

"Yes, and then they just vanished."

"What do you mean, *vanished*?"

"They put the last surveillance camera out of action."

"Play the tape, man!"

It was unmistakable. There they were, running down the corridor, four people in white coats, two of them wheeling Loratu on a trolley. One was obviously Dalziel. At the last moment, one of them turned. Just before she aimed her gun at the security camera, despite the medical mask and hat she wore, he knew at once who it was.

"Camille Blanche," Berbek whispered under his breath. The face of Mehmet came back on screen.

"We're doing all we can to…"

"Never mind all that. Find Curtis, put him up against a wall and shoot him. I want Loratu found *today,* or you'll go the same way."

He cleared the screen. He leant back and swivelled his chair round until he was facing the large painting of Britannia he'd liberated from the Tate Britain Gallery. He brought his two index fingers together underneath his top lip, and gazed at her. Then, with a heavy sigh, he turned back to the screen and tapped out a code.

The slowly flapping Union Jack logo cleared to the face of Preston, who exclaimed, "Well, I never, three times in one week! What is it this time, Garvie?"

Berbek brought his face close to the screen. He hated anyone using his first name.

"You know that girl you've got locked up in sector three?"

"Oh, you mean Loratu's girlfriend? Veema what's-her-name – Price?"

Berbek winced. He didn't find Preston's affected scattiness at all appealing.

"Can you arrange for her to – er – *escape*?"

Preston chuckled and brought his face close to the screen. "Lost him, haven't you?"

Berbek sucked in his lips. "There has been some incompetence, yes."

"Well, I don't know. I'm having such fun with her. Pretty little thing."

"Just do it," Berbek said angrily.

"She's not under your jurisdiction, you know."

"I don't care whose jurisdiction she's under. Let her go."

"All right, all right. You owe me one, remember?" Curtis's face disappeared and the screen went blank. Berbek went on staring at it. Insufferable man! Then, the right side of his mouth twitched. What was it they said? 'Don't get mad – get even.'

★ ★ ★

Moss heard far off footsteps on concrete and the banging of doors. He opened his eyes. Overhead was a white, arched ceiling; the whiteness was not uniform. Showing through it were patches of sandstone coloured rock. The paint wasn't sticking to it very well. He heard what sounded like a chair scraping, and slow footsteps approached. A woman's face looked down at him. Her grey-green eyes sparkled with what could be recognition. Something stirred in his mind, but it was quickly gone. Her pale face was suffused with anxiety, and mired with grime and sweat. Her short, black hair was cut, helmet-fashion, in a line above the ears. She turned away from him and rubbed her right eye with the back of her hand. When she turned round, her face had settled back into a mask of professionalism and command.

"We thought we'd lost you," she said in a steady voice.

"Who am I?" He asked.

She sighed heavily. "You really don't know, do you?"

"No, dammit, I don't!" He tried to sit up but couldn't move. "Why are you restraining me?"

"We're not restraining you. How do you feel?"

"Very tired and as if I'm resting on a current of warm air, and am suspended in water at the same time."

"I wondered what it would feel like."

"What would what feel like?"

"You're in a time jacket," she said, simply.

* * *

It was, Moss thought, late afternoon when she came back. The sun had worked its way round the room and was now taking on a reddish tinge. She had washed and tidied herself up but still wore the same black trouser suit, or perhaps, she had several?

"What time is it?" He asked.

"Here, have this," she said, unclasping a brushed aluminium chronometer from her wrist. "I've got another."

"Thank you very much."

"Don't thank me; you gave it to me."

"Ah, so you part with my gifts that easily?" He tried to laugh, but his ribs hurt.

"How much do you remember?" She asked, sitting down on the floor by the bed.

"Nothing," he said miserably.

"Nothing at all?"

She was beginning to irritate him.

"Oh, for God's sake! I just wish people would stop saying that. And, when do I get out of this thing?"

"Time jacket."

"*Yes*. What is it supposed to do?"

"I don't know the physics of it, but it speeds up the healing process."

Moss sighed with exasperation. She either wouldn't, or possibly couldn't, explain what the jacket's purpose was really meant to be.

"Can you get me some water?"

"Of course."

She got up and moved out of his line of sight. He heard the gurgle of water and the clink of glass.

"Here," she said, bending over him and holding the drink to his lips. He was aware of her heady perfume. With long, slim fingers, she smoothed his hair back from his sweating forehead. He noticed her nails were broken and ingrained with dirt.

"A girl can't do a proper job and have beautiful nails," she said, having noticed that he was studying her hands.

"So, what is your proper job?"

"I'm your bodyguard and your second-in-command."

"Now, or always?"

She sat down on the floor again. "In the past and, I hope,

in the future, unless you're thinking of replacing me."

"Are you any good?" As he said it, he thought, Oh, shit, that sounds really rude.

"You want me to turn somersaults and shoot from a crouching position at a target no bigger than a fly, like in the vids?" She asked sarcastically.

"No. I'm sorry." I deserved that, he thought.

"Don't be. Anyway, you used to think I was good. You know that this is as difficult for me as it is for you, don't you?"

I doubt it, he thought.

"To see you penned up here, when you… If I ever meet those bastards that did this to you, they'll have to live without testicles; that is, if I let them live." She got up and went to lean on the windowsill, her back to him, looking out through a metal grille.

"What's out there?" Moss asked.

"Branches, sky, hills."

"Where is this place?"

"We're in some caves. You used to come here to think and plan your next move, when we had decisions to make."

"This is very well appointed for a cave!" He said, trying to lighten the conversation, which certainly needed it.

She turned round and regarded him half seriously. "Have they done something to your speech patterns? You never used sound like this."

She's done it *again*, he thought. "I don't know, I don't know!" He shouted angrily, immediately wincing at the pain in his chest.

"I must stop this," he heard her say to herself. "There are two things we must do: first, get you back to health; second, we educate you. I'll arrange some physiotherapy as soon as you're well enough. Meanwhile, get some rest. I'll wheel the vid machine over, and you can watch it whenever you feel like it. Here's the remote control."

Moss watched seemingly endless vids, about the wonders of the Genome Project, interspersed with other news. It became very clear that all of the broadcasts had been carefully slanted and edited to present the best side of things for public consumption. Britain was now merely an offshore island outside the vast European bloc and was, quite obviously, a dictatorship. The only channel was "ENGLISH TV," always announced by an undulating Union Jack superimposed on a picture of sunlit fields and woods.

The Project had given the state tremendous power to manage the economy, crime and the population, but even he could see that it hadn't completely worked. Some people still wanted to run their own lives, and shape their own destinies. The Stunts, a name applied now to those people who had escaped state intervention, or whose parents had refused to conform to state control over the birth of their children, were growing in number. They could not see the advantage of being able, by choice, to give birth to perfect, blond Nordic children. Someone called Loratu had given them purpose. This was the man the government were hunting, but his picture never appeared in any of the recordings, which Moss found strange.

There were a few unlabelled disks lying on the equipment stand, and Moss, bored with the news, slid one into the machine. A big, Negroid man with grey, frizzy hair, and wearing an impressive military uniform, was being interviewed. The rows of medals on his chest glittered under the television lights. He leaned forward and seemed to look out of the picture, directly at Moss.

"I want to tell you now that no effort will be spared to find this terrorist. It is for the good of all of us."

A voice off-screen said, "And how do you propose to do this, General?"

"We already have aerial surveys. Troops are conducting a house-to-house search on an unprecedented scale. It is only a matter of time."

The camera panned over a hugely swollen Thames, glinting under an azure sky. He gasped, horrified. Where were the Houses of Parliament, and the South Bank complex? Aerial views of London, relating to the hunt for Loratu and other terrorists, showed a changed City. The London Barrage was in ruins. The low-lying lands to the east were largely submerged; tall buildings in the Docklands area had been seriously damaged, and the ruins rose above the water, like broken spikes standing in mercury. He could see the heat haze rising in a vast curtain.

Moss slept.

★ ★ ★

The door opened and the person he thought of as the Lady in Black entered. He still hadn't asked her name and, for some reason, she hadn't volunteered it. She seemed to have been avoiding him for past few days. He wished he could remember who she was. *It's time I made a good impression on her*, he thought.

"Hello, am I glad to see you," he said.

She nodded, but her expression remained serious.

He turned back to the screen, where there was a talking head. "Who's that?" he asked.

"General Berbek, Head of the Armed Forces and Counter Terrorism," she replied. "You seem to have forgotten that he is, effectively, the Government."

Moss's lips moved, testing the sound. "Berbek." He shook his head. "No, I don't remember him."

"But your gut instinct probably does," she said.

The screen flickered and showed flames pouring from the huge, rectangular windows of a darkened building. A reporter said, "This was the scene today at the Ministry of Pensions in south London. Irreplaceable records have been destroyed, putting millions of pensioners and future pensioners at risk of poverty. If you think those rebels against authority, who call themselves The People of the Mist, are fighting for you, think again."

The Lady in Black punched a button and the picture froze.

"That was just an abadoned warehouse that Berbek's men had set on fire. There is nothing wrong with the Ministry of Pensions, apart from the massive fraud that will see the people in penury."

"How convenient," said Moss. "Who are these People of the Mist?

"They are us and you are our leader."

"Don't be ridiculous!"

She pressed the button again. The picture swam fuzzily as the camera panned way from the building and zoomed in on a running figure. The focus resolved onto the upper body of a man, and then his indistinct face. Moss turned to the woman.

"That could be anyone," he said dismissively.

"But, you don't remember anything, do you?"

"No. But…"

"You're right; you were never there. The camera may not lie, but computers have no moral sense. They make lies out of truth, depending on who's operating them.

The voice-over continued. "This is the man we want, for this crime and countless others." A head and shoulders shot of a man in his early forties appeared; he had thinning brown hair and a moustache. Moss's fingers went straight to his upper lip.

"Good God! That's me!"

"We all know him, don't we? They call him Loratu. We call him an arsonist, murderer and rapist."

I can't take this anymore, he thought. "Switch it off," he shouted.

The Lady in Black didn't move.

"Now, we've got someone that he wants; someone he cherishes. If you are out there, Loratu, and watching this, we want you to know that time is on our side."

The face dissolved into that of dark-haired young woman. Her large, brown eyes had smudges of fatigue under them. She wiped her small, tip-tilted nose with the back of her hand, and said hoarsely, "Give it up. You can't win. You know they'll get us all in the end. You must stop the killing now."

The newscaster looked up and explained, "That was Loratu's girlfriend, Veema Price, captured during the firebombing of the pensions building you just saw. Remember this man." Moss saw his face flash up again. "With your help, we can catch him, and stop the killing."

This isn't really happening, he thought. I'll wake up in a minute. I will; I know I will. Dimly, he heard the transmission finally end.

"Now you know what you're up against," said the Lady in Black.

He cleared his throat. "Have they really got her?"

"Yes."

"Did she really say those things?"

"I don't know. It could all have been a computer simulation."

"How old is that transmission?"

"About two months old."

He felt sick, pulled in a deep breath, and let it out slowly.

"What do you expect me to do?"

"I want to show you something," she said, extracting the disk from the machine and substituting another. "This is the man General Berbek is looking for."

The screen showed a grim-looking man, in olive green fatigues, sitting on a bed. She paused the picture.

"No! This can't be happening. That's me again!"

"You are Loratu, our leader."

"*What*?" He'd never led anyone in his life!

"You said you couldn't remember anything."

"I don't believe it!"

"You must believe it. Everything and everybody depends upon it. Watch and learn," she said, and unpaused the picture. "I'll be back later."

He sat, gazing at the screen, hour after hour. Sometimes, he put the machine on freeze-frame, sometimes, going back and forth very slowly, until he began to believe what she had said. He didn't appear to be married nor have children because there was no reference to any close family. Nearly always, he was pictured in the company of a woman in a black trouser suit. The Lady in Black.

Occasionally, he was shown with a petite, dark-haired, young woman. In the back of his mind, there was the half-remembered image of a girl holding a placard. The two girls were one and the same. *Her* name was Veema. He felt warmth from just looking at her. The name of the Lady in Black was never mentioned.

He had been called on, and given a purpose: to fight for the outcast and disaffected. He was afraid of that responsibility, but at the same time, it gave him something to hang on to. He accepted the challenge to begin to rebuild his forgotten life. As soon as he was well enough, he would give General Berbek something to think about.

– 3 –

Veema

Veema lay back on the wooden bunk, staring at the ceiling in the tiny, white-painted cell, considering her situation yet again. She'd been here, by her reckoning, for at least three weeks, ever since they'd caught her and some companions, when they were raiding a munitions dump, intending to gain much-needed weapons for her group. By that time, Loratu had been in captivity for some six months, and everyone was beginning to lose heart. She had had some idea that, as his common-law wife, she might have been able to rally them, and make a better job of trying to find him, certainly a better job than that black-clad bitch, anyway. She hadn't managed it.

She sat up and pushed back a curl from her sweaty forehead. They kept the light on all the time and temperature at around twenty-five. It was a typical interrogation technique. They'd stripped her of all her clothes, when she'd been brought in, and given her, with much sniggering, a short smock in exchange. She'd torn a strip off the hem at the back of the garment, to cover her eyes, and that had helped her get to sleep.

She returned, wretchedly, to thinking about obtaining a weapon of some kind. The small ventilator grille was too high up the wall for her, with her one and a half metres height, to reach. She couldn't drag the bunk over, as it was bolted to the floor. A hole in the floor served as a lavatory. There was a hand basin, with a photoelectric cell controlling the sporadic water spray from a tiny spigot, and that was it. There was not even a tap, to serve as a weapon, even if she could have prised it off the wall.

Having abandoned that idea, she placed the strip of cloth over her eyes, and tied it at the back of her head, to blot out the ever-present camera, high up in the corner opposite. She wondered what they would do to her next. She remembered again the brutality of Berbek's so-called medics. As far as she was aware, she had given away no useful information, in spite of the torture. The mind-block placed on her subconscious by Dalziel had held firm.

At length, the interrogators had come to a dead stop. Short of killing her, they appeared to have run out of ideas. She hoped she was still too valuable to be killed out of hand. At her last meeting with that bastard Preston, he seemed just as weary as she was. Then she had received a visit from a man she'd never seen before; a man in a white coat, whose face was, somehow, very difficult to remember. She expected some new horror that Preston had thought up. However, all the visitor had done was ask some very ordinary questions, shine a light in her eyes and depart. Indeed, the only remarkable thing he did was shake hands with her before he left, and tell her what a pleasure and an honour it was to see her. She believed he really meant it!

She was just drifting off to sleep, when she heard the tramp of boots in the corridor. She quickly took the scrap of material off her eyes, and tied it round her neck. A key was turned in the lock, and the door creaked open. A red-faced guard in a green uniform entered.

"On your feet, you."

"What is it now? "

"You'll find out," he said, leaning forward, and pulling her to her feet, with obvious relish. They marched her quickly down the corridor and up several floors, to Preston's office. The guard knocked deferentially. A high-pitched male voice said, "Come in." The guard thrust open the door and, with a shove, propelled Veema into the room, and closed the door behind her.

As usual, the two harsh, bright lights, on either side of the dark figure at the desk, made her screw up her eyes. Directly in front of her was what she feared most. It was the chair she had been manacled to, when she was naked, while the occupant of the desk directed what should be done to her. Her mouth went dry and her heart thudded. She struggled to stay upright and calm. The floor beneath her bare feet felt damp and slimy, as if slick with sweat. Then the lights went out.

She shivered. What new trick did Preston have in mind for her, she wondered. Then the light came on again; this time it was a warm, pearly glow from the ceiling. For the first time, she could see her tormentor. He sat behind a grey, metal desk, his hands lightly clasped in front of him, resting on some files. He was looking at her over steel-rimmed spectacles, his pale face and grey eyes expressionless, giving no hint of what was coming. He licked his thin lips, looked down and poured out a glass of water from a carafe. The sound of it made her realise how thirsty she was. Without looking up, he pushed it towards her.

"Sit down, Miss Price."

"I'd rather stand."

"As you wish. It's of no interest to me, but, wouldn't you

like this water?"

He looked her up and down. Veema was acutely aware of her unkempt appearance. In her mind's eye, she was a short, thin girl with dirty hair plastered over her scalp, wearing a sweat-stained smock that ended halfway down her thighs. She didn't move to pick up the glass.

"How long have you been with us now?" He began, conversationally.

"Too damned long." Her voice sounded high and strained.

"Enjoying your stay here?"

Here it comes, thought Veema. Keep calm.

"Whether you are, or not, it's about to finish," he said.

That surprised her. "You're letting me go!" She said incredulously.

"Yes. You have ceased to be useful here. Think yourself lucky that I haven't had you terminated."

"Thanks a lot," she said.

"Don't thank me. If I'd had my way... Well, we can't let you out in that state. People will say we haven't looked after you." He opened the topmost file and took out a small slip of yellow paper. "Here is a chit for some clothes." She grasped it unwillingly. "I shall miss our little chats," he said, pressing a button on his desk.

A guard came in.

"Take Miss Price down and leave her with the quartermaster on blue level. Goodbye, Veema. I expect we shall meet again. Next time I won't be so pleasant."

The guard escorted her down the corridor, into a lift and down five floors. She smiled at him ingratiatingly. He stared stonily back. Not much luck there, then, she thought.

They arrived outside the quartermaster's office and the

guard spoke into a metal grille beside the door. A tinny voice replied and, with a buzz and a click, the door opened. Veema entered the room and the door closed behind her. She looked round. The guard had not come in with her. Perhaps things were about to improve.

In front of her was a room with nothing in it but a counter; there was another door behind that. The beginnings of a plan were forming in her head. The last thing she wanted was just to be marched off the base, or wherever she was. She hoped she might learn something useful first. She tried the door behind her, which was locked, as expected. She looked around to see if there were any surveillance cameras. Nothing. So far, so good. She hitched the hem of her smock up a bit higher.

"Hello? Is there anybody there? Can we get some service in this place?"

She heard a scraping sound coming from behind the door at the back of the counter. A man in the ubiquitous green uniform emerged.

"Yes?"

"I have a chit for some clothes," she said, moving slowly towards him, holding it out, and watching his eyes fasten lasciviously on her. Then, with the courage of desperation, she reached over the counter, grabbed him by his tie, pulled him forward and, before he could cry out, chopped him expertly on the side of the neck with the edge of her hand. She let him go, and he hit the top of the counter and, with a satisfying thump, fell heavily to the floor.

She scrambled over the counter and ran to the half-open door, expecting to be challenged at any moment. Beyond it, she could see orderly ranks of uniforms, helmets and armaments, stretching away from her, under the cold glare of strip lighting.

She ran down the line of uniforms, looking for mottled green camouflage in roughly her size. She found a jacket and trousers that would do, pulled them on, and stood panting. She hadn't thought much further than this because she didn't think she would get this far. There must be an exit somewhere; probably at the far end of the warehouse. She started to move on, and her bare feet trod on something gritty. Boots. I haven't got any boots, she thought.

She moved warily down the aisle and came across stacks of high-sided, black boots with thick soles. There was no time to look for socks; she had to find the exit. On her left, she saw assorted tools on shelves. She helped herself to a heavy spanner and a cold chisel, thinking that they would be handy if anyone, or anything, tried to impede her exit from the site.

She rounded a corner and came to a dead-end, blocked by dark green double doors with the words RESTRICTED ACCESS stencilled on them in white paint.

Have I got time to investigate? This could be interesting, she thought. She made a snap decision, tried the handle; the door was locked. No surprise.

She fitted the edge of the cold chisel between the edges of the doors and heaved. With agonising slowness, the right half of the door buckled, and the lock gave. Behind the doors was not a room, but a spacious cupboard.

Inside, on shelves, were rows of boxes. She pulled one out, put it on the floor and opened it. Inside was some kind of neatly folded, off-white garment. She took it out and examined it. It was of a stretchy, very closely woven material with a metallic feel to it. It had an integral hood that would cover the whole head, with eye slits, and a grille through which to breathe. It was like a one-piece wet-suit with hands and feet attached. A plastic seal in front ran from crotch to throat. A belt was fitted to the garment by loops at the waist. Attached to the belt were four power packs, with short leads that were plugged into the suit. At the bottom of the box were boots of the same colour.

Afraid of what might happen, but intrigued, she pressed a switch on one of the packs. The colour of the garment changed and took on a mixture of the surrounding colours. She lowered it back into the box, at which, the colour changed to the same shade as the inside of the box. Beginning to understand its properties, she pulled it out into the open again, and watched as its colour once again approximated to that of its surroundings. This was a find and no mistake! She had never seen anything like it. What a prize it would be, to bring back to the group! Replicated, a whole army could hide itself in this type of gear.

She had no time to see whether the suit would stretch over her jacket and trousers, and so she quickly undressed, unlaced her boots, and stuffed them into the cabinet. She pulled on the strange, one-piece suit, and closed the belt. She was about to turn the switch on again, when she noticed that a needle in a panel on the nearest pack was in the red sector. One of the other four was also flickering in the same area. If it meant that, together, all four were only charged up to half of maximum, or less, she hoped it would be enough to see her off the premises, at least. She would have to be sparing with the power once she was out of here.

She pressed the switch. Instantly, she was enveloped by an unpleasant tingling feeling. She felt hot and as if she were suffocating, and her vision seemed to swim. She peeled back the headpiece. The whole suit had taken on the colour of its surroundings. She was still deciding what to do next, when electronic alarms awoke with a deafening clamour.

Doors slammed somewhere, and she heard the sound of studded boots on concrete. Shouting men were coming towards her. She had to get out of this dead end. She ran up one aisle and doubled back down the next one, which was blocked by a brick wall. She pulled the headpiece roughly over her head and spread-eagled herself against the wall.

A soldier came running towards her. She closed her eyes and tried not to breathe. The footsteps slowed and stopped. She could hear his breathing, close enough for her to know that he was looking right at her. She tensed, waiting for him to call the others. He seemed to hesitate, and then he turned away.

"Nothing here, Sarge!"

She couldn't hear the reply, but he went.

Cautiously, she looked from left to right. There was a door in the far corner, to her right. As quietly as possible, she made her way over to it, and tried to turn the knob, but it wouldn't budge. She looked about her, and saw, high above, a catwalk, and over that was a darkened window. How was she to get up there? Further along, about thirty metres away, was a ladder, clamped to the wall. She was just beginning to move towards it, when she heard a shout.

"Sarge! I've found something!"

"What is it?"

"Special weapons locker's been broken open, sir!"

"Shit! If she's learned how to operate it, she could be anywhere. If she moves, there will be a slight shimmer in the surroundings. If you're near enough, and looking in the right direction, you might see it. That's what to look for."

She heard that, it was useful information. She took it to heart, ran for the ladder and began to climb, her arms aching more and more at each heave up the widely-spaced rungs. At last, breathless and giddy, she flopped onto the metal catwalk; the front power packs clanged on the surface. The sound seemed magnified, this close to the ceiling, as it echoed around the huge hall.

Shouts followed immediately, and she could see the hunters pounding towards her. She risked raising herself and looked towards the window.

"There she is!"

A volley of gunfire blazed over the top of her, showering her in brick dust. Their angle of fire was too acute. But, as she stretched out her arm, she realized the dust had made her slightly more visible. Already, one soldier was climbing the ladder. In a crouching run, she made for the window. Below her she could see a floodlit yard. Parked lorries, with tarpaulin-covered roofs, were marshalled in it. There was one of these vehicles beneath the window, its motor running.

Another burst of gunfire smashed the window. Below, the lorry's engine roared as it began to back away. It was now or never. Still crouching, she bashed the remaining shards from the frame, tucked herself into a ball, and fell out sideways onto the roof of the lorry. The canvas absorbed most of the impact, but the metal ribs supporting it momentarily winded her. As the vehicle swayed, she dug her fingers into the canvas cover and lay face down.

The lorry came out of the yard just as she heard shouts and other vehicles starting up, about to give chase. She raised her head and saw she was travelling through darkened countryside. Defoliated trees stood gaunt against the last rays of a blood-red, setting sun.

As the lorry slowed down for a particularly tight bend, she tensed and rolled off the roof, as she been taught countless times, landing in long grass beside the road. She got up and limped into a ditch, just as the first of the pursuing vehicles roared past in a splatter of mud, horn blaring, headlights full on. Another passed, packed with troops.

As they disappeared round the bend, she checked the power in the packs. It was already alarmingly low. She switched the power off and felt the tingle in her body disperse. Ignoring the pain from her bruises as well as she could, she began to half-walk and half-run across the field that bordered the road. She had no clear idea where she was going, but she knew she must put as much distance between her and her pursuers as possible, while darkness lasted.

★ ★ ★

Moss was getting used to the dry heat of the sandstone cave. There was a constant background hum from the humidifiers. Light came from a panel bolted to the ceiling, its trailing wires disappearing through a hole. It was all very amateurish, except for the metal door, set squarely in a box-like, gleaming frame that obviously meant business. There was no handle, or lock, visible on his side.

It seemed he had exchanged one prison for another, with a different bed, chair and bedside table and carafe of water, but it was still a holding pen. Why all the secrecy? Who, or what, did they not want him to see? Apart from the Physiotherapist and the Lady in Black, he saw no one. They never left the door open, when coming in or going out.

At a loss for something to do, he turned on the vid again. The recordings showed how the Genome Project had been subverted into an attempt at total control. He felt utterly sickened by what he saw. The DNA map gave insurance companies power over whom to insure, whom to load the premiums against. People thought they could see into the future, and felt that they had nothing to which they could look forward with any pleasure. A sense of crawling futility invaded the lives of most of them.

It was on the back of this public pessimism, and the changes brought about by global warming, that the Party of Regeneration had come to power. Promising to repatriate all the Temporary Islanders, incarcerated behind barbed wire in vast camps in the southwest, and to give everyone a common purpose, the Party had touched a raw nerve. "Round 'em up and ship 'em out" had been the cry. It had promised to catch criminals faster, stamp out disease, and stop wastage of resources. The Party's promise to rid the country of those who had come pounding at Great Britain's door, and the doors of Fortress Europe, and direct resources: that was the key to its success. Slowly, it had begun to say who should be spared, at both ends of life. Parliament became emasculated, and gradually ceased to function. A man called Berbek took over and the military were in control.

Ghettoes grew organically, and, with them, the power of the armed forces to control their communities. Out of the escalating chaos, a man called Loratu had welded together a fighting force to oppose the counter terrorists, and The People of the Mist group was formed. He, Moss, was supposed to be their leader, but he still remembered nothing. Every day, the thought of his responsibilities terrified him. What would happen when the group found out that he was useless?

Moss rubbed his eyes. At that moment, the door swung open and the Lady in Black came in.

"When are you letting me out?"
"Not yet."

"Why not?"

"Because."

"Look, I'm fed up with being cooped up here. Since you let me out of the time jacket, I want to be up and doing."

"Doing what exactly?"

"I don't know," he said weakly.

She switched off the vid and sat next to him on the bed.

"As you don't remember me, and nothing seems to jog your memory, we thought of trying to rescue Veema, to see if she might be able to help you. We've heard now that she's escaped, or been let go. We don't know which. No one has a clue about where she is. She hasn't contacted any of our people. It's as if she's vanished into the landscape. If we don't find her soon, I don't know what we're going to do, if we are to restore your memory. You're very important to us. Without you, the resistance movement will die. General Berbek is winning the propaganda war. Anyway, the group can't see you in your present state. You are the leader, after all."

"I just wish I could remember all this stuff. Why don't you replace me?"

"Yes. Fine, if we could, but what choice have we got?" she asked. "We've even heard that Berbek is planning to put you on trial, saying you've been captured."

"What!"

"Well, as you're not showing yourself, they can do and say what they like."

"Bit of a dilemma isn't it?" he said grimly. What ideas do you have, if any?"

– 4 –

Entrapment

It was midday. The sun beat down on a scorched landscape, and sparkled on the river lying in its valley, where it opened out to enter the sea. High tide was backing up and covering the mudflats. From far off, Bartok could hear the seagulls, on the cliffs on the opposite shore, crying as they took off and landed. Up here, it was cooler under the stunted trees. Below him, the yellow blossoms of the gorse bushes were wilting and turning gradually brown in the heat. There was scant cover among the thick tufts of yellowing grass. Elnac shuffled towards him, bent double, under the cover of the camouflaged trench. He lay down next to Bartok and looked over the lip of the earth wall.

"Seen anything?"

"Nar," said Bartok, wiping his bulbous nose with the back of his hand. "That thing you stole – done any good, then?"

"I dunno. She jus' took it, din' she? The Black Woman," said Elnac.

"How'd she talk you inter comin' 'ere, then?" asked Bartok.

"Same as you, I 'spect. Regular food. Better lodgin's. Gave me a great spiel about how the resistance needed people like me."

"Yer; layabouts."

"You watch your tongue," said Elnac.

"She said the same thing ter me," said Bartok.

"There you are, then. Give us them binos."

"Where's yours gone, then?" asked Bartok.

Elnac grinned.

"'Ere you are," said Bartok, resignedly, "but only for a bit, mind."

Elnac grasped the heavy, camouflaged binoculars in his scrawny hands and lifted them to his eyes. The computer-assisted lenses adjusted automatically to Elnac's sight, and brought everything into sharp focus. He scanned the hillside slowly.

"I don't like the way all the cover's dying back. The more it does, the more it'll be easier to find us," he said.

"They're not moving him 'til he's better," said Bartok.

"Make that soon," said Elnac. "I'm getting the jitters." He let out a long, thin breath.

"What?" asked Bartok, instantly alert.

"That bit of hillside I'm looking at keeps on waverin'."

The lenses automatically zoomed in on what Elnac had seen. Slowly and painfully, something small and blurred was moving up the hillside towards them. He scanned the hillside for further signs of movement, but there was nothing. The blur paused. Elnac switched over to heat-sensing and bio-medic mode. The heat picture showed a very hot, small female, whose heart rate was way up.

"Let's have a look," said Bartok, seizing the glasses.

"I've heard about this – but I thought it was only experimental."

"It's good, innit?" said Elnac.

"Too bloody good. How many more have they got?"

"Not many more, I hope, otherwise we're buggered."

"Who do you think it is?" asked Bartok.

Elnac pursed his lips. "See if it's one of ours, first," he said.

Bartok pressed the button for the computer to scan all known female operatives. "Got her," he said.

"Yer, so?"

"It's Veema!"

"But she's in jail, sector three," said Bartok.

"Not any more."

"I don't like it. What do we do now?"

"Report in and wait," said Elnac.

"You're taking a lot on yourself, ain't yer?"

"Well, you tell Sarge, then."

Bartok just looked at him. Elnac switched on his throat mike and spoke briefly into it, then listened to the reply in his earpiece. "He says to keep tracking her movements and wait. They've already got a lock on her."

"Nice of them to let us know," said Bartok.

Slowly the blur came closer. Elnac continued anxiously scanning the hillside for other signs of movement, but nothing showed.

"You see that dip between those two trees?" he said. "She seems to be making for that. We'll meet her there. You take the left. I'll take the right."

"Who're you givin' orders to?" asked Bartok.

"All right, what d'you want to do?"

"Oh *all right*," said Bartok, "but clear it first."

They waited in the cover of the trees. A fly buzzed round Elnac's short-cropped, sweaty head, and he swatted it expertly. Into the harsh light, under the overhanging green branches, a sun-dappled, humanoid shape wobbled, furtively weaving from side to side. Elnac made a twittering sound, and the figure stopped uncertainly. At that moment, both recruits fired their glue guns, and a web of adhesive spun lightly out into the air and draped itself over the wavering figure, freezing it into immobility. Elnac rose grinning from his hiding place and made a thumbs-up sign to Bartok.

"Let's see what we've got." he said.

"Keep low!" warned Bartok. "Do you think she's well out of sight of the hillside?"

"Of course."

"Can you see anything moving?"

Elnac dropped on all fours and crept to the edge of the glade, scanning the hillside. "Nothin'. I told you there'd be nothin'."

"Okay. Tell Sarge we're bringing in Loratu's bit of stuff."

★ ★ ★

"Strip," said the Lady in Black to Veema.

"What?" Veema was incredulous. She stood tall, outfacing everyone in the lab.

"You heard me."

"For you?"

"Not just for me," said the woman. With an elegant wave of her hand, she indicated the two lab technicians and Dalziel, the chief medical officer.

"Get lost," said Veema angrily. "What are they doing here, anyway?"

"You either strip, or I call a couple of male soldiers in and have them do it for you."

"Wait till Loratu hears about this!" said Veema, looking savagely at the lab technicians, who had the grace to blush.

"Loratu has forgotten about you. You don't exist," said the woman, icily.

Veema's lower lip trembled and her body sagged. "You're really enjoying this, aren't you, humiliating me in front of these…"

"We don't know what Berbek's lot have done to you. I doubt you know yourself."

"You make it sound so reasonable!"

The woman came right up to her and stood tensely, looking down into her face. "Well, are you, or aren't you going to do it?"

Veema looked up at her and spat full in her face. The other woman turned to the door. "All right, have it your way," she said.

Slowly, Veema bent down, unlaced her boots, and took them off. Standing up straight, she unclasped the belt with its power packs and put it on a nearby table. She could feel the tension mounting in the room, and almost stopped again, feeling cold and afraid.

"I thought we were all on the same side," she said.

The Lady in Black said nothing, but continued to look at her unwaveringly.

Veema unzipped the suit and shrugged out of it, leaving it lying on the floor like a discarded snakeskin.

"Are you enjoying this?" she said in a small voice.

One of the technicians looked away. She turned her back on her audience and pulled her smock up over her head. I might as well be back in Preston's office, she thought. These are supposed to be my *friends*. The Lady in Black moved round to face her. She drew her long forefinger sharply up

Veema's body, through her thick, black, pubic hair, over her stomach and up between her breasts, until her hand grasped Veema's chin, and tilted it towards her. Veema stared at her defiantly.

"Your body is going to tell us everything we need to know." She looked over Veema's shoulder to Dalziel. "I want this girl x-rayed, photographed, weighed, scanned and probed. Compare her with her previous medical records. I want you to find out more about her than she knows about herself. I don't care how long you take, but you must find out if she is the slightest threat to this organization. Then, I want to know how and why she escaped; that's if she did."

★ ★ ★

Moss was looking out of the window at a fine morning in the hills, when the Lady in Black entered. He let her wait for a while, sensing her impatience. He was fed up with always reacting to her.

"We found her; or, rather, she found us."

"Who?"

"Veema Price."

"There's a lot of tension between you and her, isn't there?" he said, turning away from the window.

She was sitting on the bed. "Why do say that?"

"I can tell from the tone of your voice."

"It's not a matter of whether I like, or dislike, her. I'm just doing my job," she said.

"Yes. I'll bet, and you're loving every minute of it," he said.

She pulled a face, and paused before she said, "I – er... if you knew how..." She spread hands. "If you knew how much..."

"What?"

"It doesn't matter."

"Oh, I think it does."

"Anyway, we're trying to find out whether she escaped, or if she was just let go. If they let her go, then, trouble is on the way."

"That's blindingly obvious."

She began to say something, but looked down at her hands instead.

Moss asked, "When can I see her?"

She looked up. "Have you remembered something? "

"Yes," he lied.

She smiled for the first time in a long while. It makes such a difference to her, he thought. She's almost beautiful.

"That's wonderful," she said.

"When can I see her?"

"I don't know; later, perhaps."

"Perhaps?"

"We have to be sure she's not been sent to get you." The Lady in Black spoke seriously.

"From what I've seen, she looks *very* dangerous."

"You don't understand."

"Oh, I think I understand only too well." Moss smiled confidently.

She got up, shrugged her shoulders and began to walk towards the door. He thought of using another tack to detain her.

"What's your name? I've been meaning to ask you."

She stopped and turned back towards him. "Camille," she said softly.

"Camille what?"

"Blanche."

He began to laugh. She gave him a strange look, and asked, "Why the laughter?"

"Camille Blanche: the Lady in Black."

"Oh, I see; is that what you call me?" She turned and left the room. The door banged shut.

That didn't go as well as planned, he thought. Why do I always put my foot in it?

★ ★ ★

Moss awoke suddenly: someone had just stroked his forehead. He looked up. A girl's face was smiling down at him. It only took a moment to place her: the dark-haired girl in the vids, Veema Price, the one who was supposed to have been his lover. She was wearing a white, fluffy bathrobe.

"Hello," she said quietly, a catch in her throat. "God, I've missed you."

"I would have missed you, too – if only I could remember you."

"Then, it's true what they said, that you have lost your memory," she said, looking troubled.

"What else did they say?"

"That, for you, I might as well not exist."

"Who said that?" Already, he knew the answer. It angered him.

"It doesn't matter."

"It was Camille, wasn't it?" he said, sitting up.

"I said it doesn't matter. The important thing is that you're here now. I love you so much."

He swung his legs off the bed and held out his arms to her, wanting to take away her pain. She sat on the bed beside him, her head bowed, her hands on her lap. Quietly, she began to cry. He didn't know what to do, or say, when she was in such a state. He was overwhelmed by happiness at having her so close to him again.

"I thought I'd never see you again," she whispered.

"It's all right, I'm here now."

"But do you really know who I am?"

He smiled ruefully and replied, "You don't know how much it means to me to see a friendly face."

She sighed and asked, "Haven't they been treating you well?"

"I'm getting the feeling that I'm, maybe, a bit of a liability, but, how have they been treating you? That's much more important."

"I don't want to talk about it." She pulled away from him and looked at the Time Jacket on the back of the bedside chair. "What's this?"

"Camille tells me it's called a Time Jacket. They've only just let me stop wearing it."

"I've heard about them but I've never seen one before. They were outlawed. People used them for torture. What does it do?"

"It creates some kind of stasis field, to help the healing process. You look like you could use it, after all you've been through."

"Thanks. I'll get Dalziel to show me how it works."

They looked at each other in silence, for a moment, before Moss tried again, by asking. "So, how have they been treating you?"

"I said I don't want to talk about it."

"Please." He stretched out and grasped her hand.

"I should have expected them to do what they did. This isn't a game we're playing. This is for real. I should have realized they would treat me as though I were some kind of Trojan horse."

"I'm sorry." That was all he could think of saying. He felt wretched.

"I think they must have poked into every orifice I've got, and then some."

"Who did this to you?"

"I won't name anyone. We must protect you. I'm trying to be realistic."

"It was Camille, wasn't it?"

She nodded.

He risked putting out his hand to stroke her hair. She turned towards him and he took hold of her, hugging her tightly to him. "Don't worry, no one's going to hurt you now."

She put her arms around him and leant her head on his chest. He sat, cradling her, stroking her hair, while time seemed to slow down and stop. The warmth of her body and the scent of her skin lulled him into a half dream of stirring remembrance. The barriers in his mind began to weaken. He seemed to be on the brink of some kind of revelation, when the door into the room squeaked open and destroyed the moment. He looked up to find the Camille in the doorway. He was unable to make out her expression. Shifting emotions of what could have been pain, anger, or even compassion, flitted across her face. She turned to go.

"Wait a minute," he said. She turned back reluctantly. "You did this to her, didn't you?"

"No. We all did."

"Oh, that's too easy," he said sarcastically.

Veema stirred and looked up at him. "I think I'd better go."

He frowned at Camille and kissed Veema on the top of her head. "All right, but, if they try anything else, you must tell me, OK?"

She nodded and got up, tightening her robe around her, and picked up the Time Jacket from the back of the chair. He looked over to Camille.

"You'll see Veema gets some proper clothes, won't you?"

Camille hardly moved, but her mouth set in a hard line.

"I'll take that as a yes, then," he said. He took Veema's free hand between his own, raised it to his lips and released it, and watched as she followed the other woman out of the room. The door closed behind them. He sank back onto the bed, and stared at the ceiling, unable to think further than this moment; holding her warmth to his heart.

★ ★ ★

Dalziel looked up when Camille came into the room that he had had converted into a medlab.

"Got her locked up nice and cosy?"

"For now," she said.

"You really don't like her, do you?" He peeled off his pale grey, surgical gloves, dropped them in the bin, and rubbed the stubble on his heavy jaw. He was a big man, but his movements were surprisingly light and supple. He took the surgical cap off his short, greying hair, and began to remove his gown.

She drew in a short breath. "What's that got to do with you?"

"Camille Blanche," he said tiredly, "don't you ever go off duty?"

"No," she replied flatly.

"Well, perhaps you should. Such iron self-control is not healthy."

"I just had to be sure that the girl presented no danger to us."

"There's sure and there's sure. But, I'll admit she wasn't wired up, or had any implants, apart from that heart valve of hers."

"You're certain that her valve is not a cover for anything else?"

"As certain as I can be, without taking it out and handling it myself. She's always had a weak heart."

"In more ways than one," she snorted.

"There you go again! You humiliated her."

"You let me," she said, looking fiercely at him.

Dalziel looked at her mildly. "The buck stops with you."

"I can't see what he sees in her," she said, half to herself.

"That's *very* original; anyway, it's something *our* investigations couldn't find, and we'll leave it at that, shall we?" he said. "Look, we're all tired. Let's get some rest."

"You can rest if you like," she said. "I'm going to check on the sentries."

Dalziel sighed as she disappeared out into the corridor. "Two women, and a man who doesn't remember either of them," he murmured to himself. "What are we going to do?"

★ ★ ★

"I've brought you some outdoor clothes," said Camille, coming through the door of what Moss now called his cell.

That was certainly what it felt like.

"Progress at last," Moss said.

"It's not wise to stay in one place for too long. We're moving out of here tomorrow."

"That's fine by me."

She put the bundle of clothes down on the plastic chair by his bed.

"I'll certainty be glad to get out of this overall," he said. "It doesn't do a thing for me."

She attempted a smile.

"How's Veema?" he asked, trying to sound conversational.

Her half-formed smile instantly vanished. "OK." Her voice was level, noncommittal.

"Why were you so hard on her?"

"Don't you know?"

"Please, not again!" he exclaimed angrily.

"We had to be sure that she wasn't a Government spy, working for Berbek."

"And, I suppose that excuses what you did to her, does it?"

She breathed out slowly through her sharp nose. He noticed she looked tired and had dark patches under her eyes.

"When did you last sleep?"

"Now and then," she said dully.

"Come and sit down." He hoped she would come and sit beside him on the bed, but, instead, she moved the clothes off the chair onto the bedside table, and sat down.

"By the Saints, I'm tired!" she said suddenly, the mask slipping for a moment.

"Where are we going?"

"Back to our inland base in the hills, to regroup, and for you to meet the people who depend on you."

"I'm not sure I'm up to it."

"You've got to be."

"And you're going to help me, I hope," he said.

"Of course. It's my duty."

"No more than that?"

"Let's not talk about it anymore," she said, the mask back in place.

"Will Veema be coming with us?"

"You want that?"

"Yes."

"Then I'll go and see to the arrangements." She indicated the package on top of his clothes. "They are disks, for you to familiarize yourself with your personnel. I had them made up specially. They'll have to be destroyed before we go, so make sure you memorize them properly." She got up to leave, then added, "We move out under cover of darkness, tomorrow night, at twenty-two hundred hours. Goodnight."

After she had left, he spent several hours trying to remember what the people he was supposed to command looked like. It was difficult. Eventually, when he felt that he could keep his eyes open no longer, he had a shower and went to bed.

★ ★ ★

Veema woke up with the memory of a man's voice quoting poetry. She heard footsteps quietly moving away from the door to her cell. She got up and was just in time to see through the reinforced glass the back of someone going round a corner, but she wasn't sure who it was. She looked at her watch. Twenty-five past midnight. The bitch, Camille, had briefly allowed her to visit her own quarters, to collect some clothes and a few personal possessions, like her watch and the thin, gold, neck-chain Loratu had given her. She wore this defiantly, openly, just to see the bitch's expression. Then, under armed guard, she'd been escorted back to the cell, carrying her belongings and the Time Jacket in a shoulder bag.

This cell wasn't going to hold her for long. One of her greatest assets was an excellent photographic memory. She had now seen the door keypad operated twice, and she thought she could reproduce the hand movements. Of course, if this had been a real holding cell, there wouldn't have been a pad on the inside, but they had used a secure storage room that could be locked from both inside and outside, "just temporarily", so Camille had said, while they finished their tests on her.

She quickly pulled on a combat jacket and trousers over her underwear. It took her a moment to finger the keypad before the lock clicked open. Barefoot, she crept out into the corridor, listening for the slightest sound. She hoped everyone would be asleep, except, of course, the guards on the outside, who were keeping watch for intruders. She was going to see HIM, whatever happened, without that bitch intervening. Silently, she followed the maze of corridors. On arriving outside his bedroom, she pressed the entry pad. She hadn't been able to see how this was operated, when they had brought her down, because the door was already open. There must be a code for him as well. Think girl! Think! What would they use? His name? Too obvious. His own code word had been his real name, MOSS, but, surely, they would have changed that. Perhaps part of it would do. She typed it in. Nothing. How about backwards? The lock clicked. Well, she thought gleefully, Camille was never very original.

She partially opened the door very slowly and squeezed through the small gap. She pushed the door to, so that it looked closed from a distance. A faint radiance came from the open archway to the bathroom, just enough to see him asleep, his naked back above the bedclothes.

Her movements suddenly became very mechanical. Her mind a blank, she moved quickly over to him. Peeling back a thin, transparent film from the surface of the nail of her little finger, she placed it on the back of his neck, where it began to dissolve quickly. The nanites, already keyed to his brainwave patterns, slipped quickly under his skin.

She turned, and, just as mechanically, left the room, closing the door behind her. The click of the lock seemed to rouse her from her somnambulistic state. She wondered momentarily what she was doing outside his bedroom, and then the memory of their lovemaking took over. That was something the bitch would never know about. She smiled, feeling warm and luxurious, and made her way back to her cell. Once inside, she fell on the bed and was instantly asleep.

– 5 –

The Gift of Tongues

"I don't like it," said Elnac, sniffing loudly. "You're always sayin' that," said Bartok. "What is it now?"

"Smell the air."

Bartok gave an exaggerated sniff. He coughed. "I don't smell nothin' unusual, apart from you, that is. You've 'ad a bath, ain't yer?"

"Shut up," said Elnac. It was too dark for Bartok to see him blush.

"I know – it's that pretty little programmer on level two. I could quite fancy 'er myself. I…"

Elnac's bony elbow hit him in his well-upholstered chest. "Quiet!" Something in the urgency of Elnac's voice cut across Bartok's lascivious thoughts.

"Well, what is it, then?" he whispered.

"Fumes of some kind; driftin' downwind," said Elnac tensely.

"You an' that famous nose of yours!"

Elnac snatched up the glasses, which were already on night-vision, and anxiously scanned the horizon all round. "I could have sworn…"

"Yer. Well, as I was sayin'…"

"Prophet's beard!" breathed Elnac.

"What? What?" shouted Bartok, now aware of a drumming sound in the air.

Elnac switched on his throat mike. "They're coming in low over the sea. I can see three, no, four, eight, maybe more."

As he said the last words, six great, bat-like shapes roared over them, across the sky. They ducked involuntarily.

"*What the hell are they?*" Bartok screamed at Elnac.

"Stealth craft. Run for it!"

The downdraught whipped up dust and dry bracken, throwing it in their faces as they fled along the hillside. A cold circle of light wavered towards them. Tracer fire whined overhead. Elnac grabbed his companion by the arm. "This way!"

"But that's away…"

With manic energy, the smaller man nearly pulled Bartok off his feet. "Only a bit further!"

There was a loud explosion overhead, and they were both knocked to the ground. Elnac was slightly dazed; without hesitation, Bartok heaved him up and supported him.

"Just over the ridge, there's a ditch," Elnac croaked.

Answering fire came from the cave mouth away from which they were running, and the wavering circle of light vanished. They made it to the lip of the ridge, and fell into the ditch.

"Crawl, you bugger," Elnac bawled. "There's a side-tunnel up ahead. That's where I have my bolt-hole."

Bartok heaved the other man into the mould smelling darkness and lay down panting heavily.

"Where's this go to?"

Elnac coughed, "Private bolt hole. Just told you that."

"What's that smell?"

"Some of my stock must have gone off."

"What do we do now?" asked Bartok.
"Keep our bloody 'eads down."

★ ★ ★

Moss woke up, dimly aware of loud booming overhead, and running footsteps, echoing hollowly in the caves. The door to his room slammed open against the stone wall. Camille was silhouetted against the light from the passage.

"We're under attack. Get out of here," she shouted from the doorway.

"What's going on?" he called after her, but she had vanished up the corridor. His head felt heavy, as if stuffed with cotton wool, but above all, he felt nauseous. Every time he moved, the room whirled round him. Somehow, he felt for his clothes and, supporting himself on the wall, pulled on the olive green trousers and shirt. He took a few steps and nearly fell over.

The pungent, gritty, smell of gunfire floated into the room. He could hear shouting and screams. The muffled explosions continued, interspersed with the stutter of automatic weapons. He staggered painfully to the door and stood leaning against it, not knowing what to do, or which way to go.

Camille came running towards him; blood from a wound over her right eye trickled down her face.

"Why the fuck are you still here? Come *on*!"

"Can't move. Feel sick."

"Put your arm round my shoulders, and let's get a move on!"

He vomited. Without a pause, she picked him up in a fireman's lift, and began to run.

★ ★ ★

Veema was awake and on her feet the moment she heard the first explosion. She deftly opened the door lock on her cell, thankful that her exceptional memory had recorded the number sequence of the locking device. She looked down the corridor. Smoke, back-lit by orange flashes, was drifting towards her from the left. First, she needed some boots, and then a weapon. She gathered up her shoulder bag, containing the Time Jacket and spare clothes, and sprinted off down the corridor. The stores were on this level. She just hoped they were not locked.

To her immense relief, the door to the storeroom was wide-open. Quickly putting on some boots, and slinging a laser rifle over her shoulder, she made for the science laboratory, one floor up. Before she left, she had to retrieve the chameleon suit that Camille had removed from her and taken there.

Now that she had something to do, she channelled her anger into doing it. She'd better not meet that bitch, she thought, or she would do her serious damage. No one would notice anything, in the din that was going on. Already she was breathing heavily as she pounded up the stone stairs. Prison life had allowed her to get out of condition. At the top the corridor turned to the left, ending in closed, steel doors. She stood still, controlling her breathing.

She didn't know the code for the storeroom doors. She unslung the rifle and considered using the butt as a tool to lever them open.

"Not wonderful," she murmured, "but it will have to do. Why not fire on the lock-operating panel? Better. I'm far enough away to be safe from flying debris."

She raised the laser rifle and pressed the trigger. A thin,

green line hit the panel, which exploded in a shower of sparks. The doors grated open about 25 centimetres, and then stuck.

Although out of condition, she was thinner than usual. She ran forward, heaved at the edges of the doors, and squeezed through into the room beyond. The chameleon suit she was after lay on a bench. Its power packs were hooked up to a supply line, and their dials indicated that they were fully charged. She felt she was due for a stroke of luck, and this was it.

Unplugging the packs, she was about to pull the one-piece suit over her jacket and trousers, when she remembered the integral boots. As she removed the ones she'd put on earlier she heard footsteps on the stairs. Through the gap between the doors, she could just see two men in black uniforms. Seizing the rifle, she quickly squatted down behind the bench and waited.

The first man pulled at the edge one of the doors. "Give me a hand with this will you? Looks like we found it."

Together, they enlarged the gap enough for them to come in one at a time.

"There it is; over there," said one.

In one fluid movement, Veema rose from behind the bench and fired at the nearest man, who screamed as the laser beam hit his chest. The other man fired at her as she weaved to her right, but his aim was poor. She fired again, and she also missed. The man took cover behind the bench. Stalemate!

She ducked and cautiously reached up, to pull the chameleon suit off the bench. An energy beam spat over her head. She heard an echoing clatter of studded boots on the stairs. She hoped it wasn't reinforcements. She chanced a look.

A pulse of green laser-light came between the doors, aimed

at her. She dropped down just in time. The man inside the room looked up and turned, momentarily, to see who it was; presenting a target to her. Her shot caught him in the shoulder. It looked as if she was in a trap, but her attacker still had to come through the doors. Whoever he was, he was taking no chances. A gas grenade sailed through the gap and landed, with a muffled thud, behind one of the benches. Choking smoke billowed towards her.

If only she could get the suit on in time... She took a deep breath and squirmed into it, while lying full length on the floor. She managed to zip it up and pull the hood over her head before the fumes reached her. She heard footsteps, and a soldier in a gas mask flitted briefly between the doors and took refuge beside one of the metal cabinets that lined the room. Judging she would be less easy to see in an off-white suit, in the smoke, she risked raising herself enough to snatch the power packs off the bench. Although they made a noise as they slid across the surface, she hoped her attacker would be too busy, peering into the murk and wondering why his prey hadn't succumbed, to notice the sound. She attached the belt to the suit, and peered round the edge of the bench.

She could see the remaining man coming forward from the cover of the cupboard, and she fired, hitting him in the chest. His arms went up, and, with a muffled cry, he fell back clumsily.

No point in taking any further risks, she thought, and switched on the chameleon suit's power pack. Instantly she felt the familiar tingling, and there was a buzzing in her ears, which quickly cleared.

There was a row of monitors to her right. She switched on all of them. They showed different views of the complex. Everywhere, there was serious fighting. She called up on a computer screen a three-dimensional schematic of the base, and fed in all the information from the surveillance cameras. Only one escape route seemed to be viable, the one to the VTOL cave, which was, for now, being defended successfully, while the base was being evacuated. She hoped she would get there before the last flight left.

★ ★ ★

Camille sprinted up the embarkation ramp to the VTOL. She unloaded Loratu into one of the two seats in the front of the cabin of the small, delta-winged craft, and leant against the doorway, to catch her breath. She was glad to think that they had got away without Veema, whose fate was of no interest whatsoever to her.

All around her, the entire base contingent was powering up for flight. Over the roar of engines came the sound of metal grating on metal, as the giant iris diaphragm of the exit hatch opened, showing fading stars speckling the early morning sky.

The great underground cavern was full of the reek of smoke and the glare of afterburners. There came the muffled thump and fizz of gas grenades that were being lobbed over the heads of the defenders, who were grouped around the tunnel entrances. Others were firing from the gantries clinging to the rock wall. A scene from hell.

Just before Camille raised the aircraft loading-ramp, she thought she saw something like a heat haze appear at the doorway and then disappear. She dismissed it out of hand, as the hatch way hissed closed. Red, back-lit smoke rolled across the cabin window as a detonation rocked the craft on its landing gear. She could dimly hear screams. She punched instructions into the navicom. Several craft took off in front of her and headed for the exit.

Agonisingly slowly, the VTOL rose from the rock floor, and wavered like a leaf caught in the wind. A metallic, computer voice imposed itself over the muffled din outside. "Warning. Exit hatch closing in 20 seconds."

Camille looked across to where Loratu lay sprawled.

"Strap yourself in. This is going to be fucking close."

He didn't move. She had no time to care. She strapped herself to her seat and took over manual control, putting the machine into a steep corkscrew incline, her fingers dancing over the lighted panels.

"16 seconds."

"Alright, you stupid thing!"

They weren't going to make it. The black iris diaphragm was closing too fast.

"Contract the wings," said a female voice.

What the hell? I know that voice, she thought. It's Veema. How the hell did she get aboard! It was her voice, all right. What's more, she knew what she was talking about. Camille hit the auxiliary power and wing control simultaneously. In a burst of smoke and flame, the VTOL screeched through the aperture. The smell of burning filled the cabin, but they were free, out in the open air.

The tactical readout showed two fighters bearing down on them from the southwest.

"Have you got the shield powered up?" Veema asked.

Camille squirmed round in her seat, her harness tugging hard across her chest.

"Where are you, Veema?"

"Right behind you, at the auxiliary controls. Now, will you *please* get that shield up?"

"*Alright*, but I don't see what good it's going to do. They can still see us."

"They won't in a minute, if I'm right," said Veema, "but launch a heat-seeking missile, and get those wings extended before we fall out off the sky."

"You'd better have a bloody good explanation for this," said Camille, puzzled. She set the missile running.

"Raise the shield," said Veema, "and sheer off to the right, vector 3. 633."

The craft swung giddily as it adjusted to its new course.

"That takes us down to the surface of the sea," Camille said.

"Now, cut the engines, and hug the coastline, while I see what I can do with this."

"You'll crash us," said Camille.

"Not if you do as I say," said Veema.

"How come you're such a frickin' expert, all of a sudden?"

"Shut up. You'd better hope this works."

"I feel peculiar," said Camille. "It's as if I've got pins and needles all over."

"Rather that, than be blown out of the sky."

Camille Blanche saw again the strange heat haze effect that she had noticed as she was about to take off. This time, it was shimmering in front of the cabin window.

"What have you done?"

"You didn't see me, when I came on board, did you?"

Light dawned for Camille. "You're piggybacking the shield signal with the chameleon system that you stole."

"Correct. Are they still following?"

"No. They went after the heat source. Now, they're just cruising around. We can't go on gliding for much longer.

The water surface is getting awfully close."

"They're not far enough away yet." said Veema.

"We'll have to risk a little lift," Camille said.

"All right, behind the next headland, but make it short."

"We're going to have to ditch this thing, eventually, with so many enemy craft about," said Camille.

"Loratu used to speak of a deep lake somewhere around here, caused by collapsed mine workings, but he never gave me the co-ordinates," said Veema. "You'd better ask him how we get there."

Camille glanced over at Moss. "He's asleep."

"Wake him up, then." hissed Veema.

Camille leaned across and shook him. "Wake up," she urged.

Moss's eyes flickered open. "Half past twelve," he said.

"What are the coordinates of the old lake? You told me once that your father and you used to fish there when you were a boy."

"Chocolate cake with a lot of sugar."

Camille felt her scalp crawl.

"This is no time for mucking about. Where's the bloody lake?"

"Half of one and six dozen of the other."

Camille bent down low to him and spoke deliberately. "Moss, you are not making sense. This is urgent."

"Let me try," said Veema. "Darling, do-you-remember-the-Lake?"

"Nonesuch?"

"What?" said Camille. She shook him. Her mouth had gone very dry. What the hell was the matter with him? "Talk sense, man!"

Moss's face contorted with the effort of speaking.

"What-mouse-went-up-the-tunnel?" he said carefully.

Camille shook her head.

"It's no good; there's something very wrong with him."

She could see him struggling to form a reply. Beads of sweat stood out on his forehead. He put his hand to his mouth as he spoke, fingering his lips, as if he could not believe the words they were forming.

"I bridged that mouse up the tunnel," he shouted, sitting bolt upright and hitting the chair arm with his fist.

Camille looked round to the auxiliary control desk, her skin cold.

"What the hell do we do now?"

– 6 –

The Worms Turn

The tunnel was airless and clammy. A tree root was sticking into Elnac's back. Bartok was breathing fast.

"What's the matter?" Elnac whispered.

"Don't like small spaces."

"We'll be out soon. Hey! Can you hear anything?"

"No," Bartok gasped. Then he began to cough.

"Quiet!"

"Can't help it."

Heavy footsteps overhead brought soil showering down from the tunnel roof.

"You, down there, come out slowly."

Bartok squirmed around to face Elnac.

"You got a back door to this place?"

"Nar."

"On the count of three," shouted a voice. "One... two... three."

"Let's see you get us out of this one," said Bartok.

Elnac grunted, trying to think of something. It would best to wait until they were outside and had more information. He began to scrabble his way up the incline, towards the now lightening sky.

Emerging, he saw six or seven infantrymen surrounding the entrance. There were more in the background. No point in heroics, then. He struggled to his feet, hearing Bartok growl behind him. He hoped an opportunity for escape would present itself, and soon.

"Clasp your hands behind your heads. Move."

He felt something prod sharply into his back.

They were marched up over the lip of the hill. Below them, a large stealth craft and a small, delta-winged shuttlecraft stood on a grassy shelf between two rocky outcrops, close to the cliff's edge. Elnac looked up. Two stealth craft were flying away to the west, over the sea. He was pushed down the slope and on to the flat ground near the larger craft.

"Stop."

A hatch in the craft cracked open and a large man in green battledress strolled down the ramp, his stomach bulging over his tightly belted trousers. Short, white hair clung fungus-like to his dark skin. Berbek, thought Elnac. That's all we need.

General Berbek swaggered slowly up to the sergeant in charge of the group, slapping a gold-crowned rod against his open left palm. The sergeant saluted smartly.

"Found these hiding in a foxhole, sir."

"Ah, yes. Elnac, the thief, and his sidekick, Bartok, the thicko. I've heard *so* much about you. Well, well..." He looked at the ground and then full in Elnac's face. "You'll be pleased to know that your beloved leader has got away; doubtless, to do more damage than you could possibly imagine. You, meantime, will be going to Anglesey, where I hope you will be equally useful. Put them in the shuttlecraft hold."

Elnac's heart thumped. Once on that fortified island, they'd never leave.

The hold was chilly, dark, and gritty underfoot. His wrists were strapped together with something that felt like plastic. He imagined the same was happening to Bartok. They were made to sit back-to-back, and were bound together round their chests. Then, Elnac's feet were strapped together with the same material. The soldiers left them, and the hold door clanged shut, leaving them in complete darkness.

"I don't think I can take much more of this," Bartok said in a low voice.

"Don't worry, we'll soon be out of here."

"You said that before." Bartok's voice was still edgy.

"As long as they put the lights on."

"I sure hope you're right."

The air around them began to thrum. The darkness was full of metallic creaking and groaning. Elnac felt the shuttlecraft lifting off the ground. At the same time, two green lights came on, and he could see again. He breathed a sigh of relief, as much for himself as Bartok.

"Pull my shirt out of the back of my trousers." he said.

"What?"

"Just do it."

"'Ere, you're not one of them, are yer?" said Bartok.

"Oh, for Prophet's sake! Did you ever see carbon fibre slice through things?"

"Nar."

"Well, you will, if only I can get the hem of this shirt open."

He felt along the ridge at the bottom of the material at the edge of his shirt, and began to tear at the stitching. With a feeling of triumph, he closed his thumb and forefinger on the thread hidden in the hem. Gingerly, he drew it out and felt for Bartok's wristbands.

"Hold your wrists steady and your hands as far apart as you can. I'm going to saw through your wristbands." If I can, he thought.

It seemed to him that it took an age before he managed to make an impact on them. He fervently hoped they weren't travelling too fast; otherwise, they would land on Anglesey before they got free.

"Try and drag your wrists apart. That might break the strapping."

He heard Bartok grunting. "Done it," he said.

"Right, you do the same for me. It should be easier now you can move your hands. Thread the fibre down behind the wristband and saw through it."

It didn't take so long this time. Elnac brought his hands round to the front of his body and Bartok sawed through the strips holding his legs, and then the band round both their bodies. By the end, even Bartok's horny skin was beginning to bleed, from holding the ends of the fibre looped round his fingers. He hid his pain from Elnac. One of them had to appear to be in control. Elnac shook his fingers, to restore his circulation.

"So far, so good. How do we get out of this bloody hold?"

"With the aid of this, my friend." Elnac picked open his left cuff and produced a square of what looked like stiffened cotton with circles and other markings on it.

"What's that?"

"Smart material."

"Where'd you get that, then?"

Elnac screwed up his eyes and grinned. "You name it, I can steal it. This has saved my bacon on more than one occasion." He went over to the door and placed the smart material on the wall next to the keypad. "These places aren't meant to be prisons. Should be out in no time." He pressed a couple of circles on the material.

"What's it doing?"

"Cycling through thousands of door-lock combinations." He put his ear to the lock. His acute hearing picked up a barely audible click. "Yesss! Right. Follow me. Let's see who's flying this thing."

"D'you know how to fly it?"

"No, but I'm a quick study." *I hope I am*, he thought; *otherwise, we've had it.*

"Sounds great," mumbled Bartok. "You got that carbon thing?"

"Of course."

Bartok smiled broadly. "Good for throats as well, is it?" He drew his fingers across his throat in an unmistakable gesture.

"Here you are, then. Garrotting is rather more your department."

"Ta."

"I'll go up the ladder first. You follow quietly, and I mean *quietly,* OK?

Elnac deftly mounted the steel rungs. As his head poked above the floor-line, he saw two men in the cockpit; they were seated in front of a Plexiglass window. Both wore helmets, which made it more difficult to get them round the throat. However, the engine noise was louder up here. Elnac bent his head down to Bartok, who was still behind him, on the ladder.

"There's two of them. You take the left. I'll take the right. The left one's the gunner. He's expendable."

He climbed the last two rungs and squatted by the access

way, while Bartok lumbered up into the cabin. Elnac gestured over to the left, and they rose simultaneously, one behind each man. Elnac's sinewy arm snaked underneath the pilot's chin; he heard a nasty crunch come from his left. Bartok had done his job. He pulled upwards.

"Where would you like to go, my friend, into oblivion, or somewhere warmer?"

The pilot tried to say something but Elnac kept his grip on the pilot's throat.

"Is this thing on autopilot?"

The pilot tried to nod.

"How long to Anglesey?"

"Can't breathe."

Elnac wasn't sure he was cut out for this rough stuff. Get in, get the loot and get out, was his motto. He'd never killed anyone at close quarters before. He risked a glance across to Bartok, who had no such scruples. The gunner lay lifeless, slumped in his seat.

"Are you on an open channel?"

Again, the partial nod.

"Turn it off."

The pilot didn't move. He needs more encouragement, Elnac thought. He looked over to Bartok and mouthed at him, "Stick a gun in his back." He knew from experience that Bartok would understand.

The big man moved over and jabbed a hard forefinger through a hole in the back of the pilot's seat, at shoulder height. Elnac spoke close to the pilot's head.

"What would you say to a nasty, but not entirely fatal, shoulder injury, my friend?"

"O.K.," the pilot wheezed.

Elnac loosened his grip, so that the man could turn off the

microphone. It was all he needed.

"Mayday. Mayday."

Instantly, Bartok's huge arm clamped round the pilot's neck. The pilot tried to struggle; Bartok merely tightened his grip, until he felt the man go limp.

"Great. You've killed him," said Elnac.

"You do know how to fly this thing, don't you?" Bartok said.

"I said I could learn," Elnac replied, under his breath. Elnac's heart was pounding. "Get him out of the seat, quick."

Bartok pulled the pilot's helmet off and put it on the console, released the safety harness, and, together, they heaved the dead weight on to the floor. Elnac sat down unsteadily in the pilot's seat and picked up the helmet. He could hear a buzz now. He put the helmet on. It felt hot and damp against his skin. The buzz became a voice.

"Blue Flight. Come in, Blue Flight. What is the emergency?"

The voice faded, as if the speaker had moved away from his microphone, to speak to someone else. Elnac heard him say, "I can't get an answer, sir. They're still on course."

A new voice, deeper and gruffer, came on air.

"What are you mucking about at, Kochansky?"

Down the sides and across the top of the visor, holographic images danced and wheeled chaotically. Elnac felt disorientated, and thought, I've got to do something fast. He put his hand over his mouth, muffling his voice.

"Nothing, sir. Momentary problem. OK now."

"Something wrong with your voice, Kochansky?"

"All right now, sir. Swallowed something the wrong way, sir."

"What have I told you about eating on duty?"

"Sir, yes, sir!"

"Carry on."

Elnac concentrated hard on the dancing figures on the visor, at last making sense of them: Heading; Height above sea level; Distance to target; Distance to target! Shit! Only ten minutes away.

First, he had to cut the automatic transmission lock. He gazed at the giddying number of touch panels in front of him.

"Got it. Disengage autopilot, and swing her back to previous heading. Child's play really." It clarified his thoughts, to speak them aloud.

"Blue Flight, why have you changed course?"

The voice in the helmet made him jump. He pushed the microphone well to the side of his mouth, and clasped his hand round it.

"We have a fuel leak. Have to return to previous heading."

"What? You have a what?"

"We have a fuel leak."

"You are very close to base now. Return to previous heading."

Elnac thought fast. "Too much headwind. Must go with wind current."

"Negative, Kochansky. Your signal is breaking up. Readjust."

Elnac made spitting and squawking sounds, and twisted the microphone stalk back and forth until it broke. That ought to fix them for the moment, he thought. He turned to Bartok, who had seated himself in the gunner's position.

"Let's see what this baby can do."

"Where are we going?"

"D'you want to give Berbek a surprise?"

"Was the Pope Catholic?... but, in this? You're off your 'ead!"

"If Berbek's still on the ground, not expecting us, and without his shields up, I'd say we'd got more than a fighting chance."

Bartok grinned. "I've always fancied having a go at these laser cannons."

★ ★ ★

General Berbek sat at his desk, in his private cabin, in the command stealth aircraft. He turned to a viewing port and glanced through it at the rearing cliff face and the sea far below. All round him, he could hear the clang of boots on steel, as the crew readied the ship for take-off. Everything else had already left the area of Loratu's hideout. It had been a successful mission. The People's base had been cleared out, and Loratu had been allowed to escape; and yet, Berbek was still very uneasy. They'd let the shuttlecraft leave, as planned, but then it had disappeared. The tracking device inside the Price girl's heart-valve told him she'd been on the move at the right time that night and, presumably, had placed the patch on Loratu's neck. But then there had been that strange interference pattern, and the shuttlecraft had disappeared – and so had the signal. If Loratu couldn't talk, that would be it, wouldn't it? And yet... suppose he remembered Project Alpha? That would be a disaster. It was nowhere near ready.

He turned his chair round to the desk again, and looked at the blank screen in front of him. His stubby fingers swiftly typed the code for the private, closed channel, and the screen lit up.

Preston came on screen, and looked up from what he was doing. His thick, oval spectacles caught the light, hiding his grey eyes.

"Hello, Garvie. What's wrong now?"

"What's the news on the Project?"

"So they got away?"

"As planned," said Berbek, unmoved.

"So they got away," Preston repeated. "Told you it wouldn't work."

"That expensive technology from Eurocom better had, though."

"Oh, it will, it will." replied Preston.

"But, for how long?"

"Long enough. It was experimental. The gradual motor neuron damage to Loratu may be irreversible. Why should you care?"

"I don't," said Berbek.

"But, all the same, you want reassurance?"

"Call it that, if you like." Berbek stared hard at him over the link.

"All we've come up with is anomalous. Loratu tampered with the time stream, before we captured him. We think he used it to send something back, before the system blew. If we could duplicate that… But, more bothersome is this interference pattern that we've had beaming in from the direction of Jupiter. It's been getting worse over the years. For a long time, it was just background white noise. Now, it's really disrupting things. Sometimes, we manage to tune it out, but… You remember that Eurocom sent a probe, four years ago, to orbit Europa, one of Jupiter's moons. The interference seems to have worsened since then. It's messing up our experiments. It's almost as if something is trying to break through from outside."

Preston's hand, which had come up to his chin, gestured vaguely.

A loud explosion jolted the ship, and the viewing port Berbek had been looking through crazed over. With a grinding of metal, the room tilted sideways, throwing him to the floor. The transmission to Preston abruptly cut off. Berbek hit the floor heavily. Before he was able to take in what was going on, the bulkhead door to the cabin slammed shut. He shook his head, to clear it. What the fuck was going on? He groped to a standing position, holding onto the fixed chair, and managed to sit down. He called up the control centre.

"What's going on?"

The pale, sweating face of Number One swam into view, against a background of smoke and flashes of light.

"Thought it was one of our own, sir. It gave all the right recognition codes. Then, it started firing on us. The captain's dead, sir."

"What's the damage to the ship?"

"Starboard sheer legs have been blown away. With the exhausts this close to the ground, we risk explosive back draft."

"Are the shields up?"

"No, sir. Main generator's knocked out. We are deploying auxiliary power."

"Are we returning fire?"

"No, sir. They found a way to lock out the missile systems for the moment."

"So, use the laser cannon."

"All auxiliary power is diverted to the shields, sir."

Berbek cursed the designers of the vessel. "Get me through

to their ship."

"Sir."

The screen in front of him cleared to a snow effect, then a weasel-like man, with a long nose, and a curtain of beard hanging off his lower jaw, appeared. It was Elnac, the safecracker. Trust him to be behind this, Berbek thought, and glared at the screen.

"What do you want?"

The man smiled, showing bad teeth. "You, Berbek," he said, and cut the transmission.

The craft lurched again. Why weren't they doing anything? Got to get the bulkhead door open. Where are the manual controls? Berbek disengaged the lock and slowly wound the handle, inching the door back, until he could squeeze his bulk through. He was going to have Number One's hide for this. Who the hell was training them these days?

By the time he found his way to the command centre, a certain degree of calm had been restored. Fire extinguishers were being used to put out the remaining electrical fires.

"Report, Number One."

"They've backed off, sir. They can't penetrate the shields on our new oscillating frequencies, but we can't move."

"So, what's your plan?"

"We're getting the aft landing jets on line to lift the tail up."

The ship began to tilt upright, shuddering. The voice of the computer cut in.

"Warning. Landing jets overheating."

"Override," shouted Berbek. "Get us out of here, dammit."

Number One winced, but didn't dare answer back. He typed in the order. The ship began to plough forward off the top of the cliff and tip towards the sea.

Number One spoke to the computer.

"Bring all jets on line and balance for the rear distortion field."

"Acknowledged."

"Have you hit it yet?" Berbek shouted to Tactical.

Number One looked up at him. "I already said...

"That's gross insubordination."

What were they teaching these lads, nowadays? he thought.

"They seem to be withdrawing," said Number One calmly, as the ship levelled out.

"I want some action!" said Berbek, slamming his fist down on the panel beside Number One.

"I think that's unnecessary now, sir."

Berbek glowered at him.

"When we get back to Anglesey, I want a full report."

As he strode off the bridge, knocking a technician out of the way as he did so, he knew he had failed to exert his authority. They were air force. He was military. He shouldn't have been such a fool as to try to enforce his will over them. He just wanted to ring that stunt Elnac's neck. He felt so bloody powerless, but he'd get him, somehow.

– 7 –

Gestalt

Moss stared at Camille. Was she clinically thick, or something? He tried again, the words forming perfectly in his head. The co-ordinates of the lake are 456 by 764, vector 843.7. That's what he thought he said, but she continued to stare blankly at him. He tried again. She turned away, looking at nothing, and spoke. This couldn't really be happening. He would try one more time, tracing his mouth movements with his finger. He thought he was speaking very deliberately. He *was* speaking gibberish. Sweat trickled down his face. Camille looked very concerned. He reached forward, took her hand, and squeezed it. That was real enough. A faint smile flitted across her face. She turned and said something, but, to him, it sounded all muddled.

He felt a tingling at the back of his neck, under his hair, and automatically put his hand up to it. Camille was on him instantly, like a tigress, parting his hair and feeling his skin. A look of comprehension spread over her face and she turned away. She spoke to someone, another woman, but he could make nothing of the conversation. Camille moved out of his line of vision.

Abruptly, an electronic note pad with writing on it was thrust in front of him. He read slowly and methodically. 'Red patch of irritation on back of neck. Think you under influence of drug. Need to find your lake, if we are to lose our pursuers. Going to put area map on screen. Point to it.'

Inexplicably, his hearing cleared enough for his brain to make out the occasional word.

"...status..."

"...think... lost... moment... can't count..." Veema's voice! But where was she?

Camille put a plastic cup of water in his hand, made drinking motions, and pointed towards the screen in the middle of the control panel. He took a long drink and watched the map scroll across the screen. There it was! He pointed. She fed the information into the navicom, and he felt the craft lift and move on to a new heading. He drained the last of the water, and gestured to her for something to write with. She handed him a stylus. He wrote laboriously on the pad, 'Where's Veema?'

"...control... into... power..."

"What?" He mouthed at her.

She grabbed the stylus and wrote quickly: 'At auxiliary controls tapped into shield using cloaking device stolen from govt.'

'Can't she come out?' he wrote.

'Manually holding system together,' she scrawled.

He held out the cup, gesturing for more water. He had to laugh. It was so laborious. He scribbled on the pad again: 'What wrong with me?'

'Someone put drug patch on back of neck.'

He put the stylus and note pad on the control panel. How long would it take to wear off?

"...for... they...?" Veema's voice was getting tired.

Camille glanced at the display. "Not... go... hang on..."

Time passed. The hum of the engines lulled him into a semi doze. There was nothing he could do, anyway. Without realising it, he fell asleep.

When he opened his eyes, the engine note had changed to a singing whisper. He felt a touch on his arm. Looking round, he saw Camille; she used her hand to imitate something floating, and pointed at the display. They must be hovering over the lake. She mouthed at him very slowly. It looked like, "What we do now?"

He grabbed the note pad and stylus from the control panel and wrote one word: 'Submerge.'

She raised her eyebrows and pursed her lips. Then, with a resigned gesture, she fed the command into the computer.

Gently rocking, the craft descended and hit the water's surface without much impact. It was a curious sensation, watching the water level rise up the view ports. The ship creaked all over. He could sense its joints taking the strain of the water pressure. Camille scribbled something more on the pad. 'Never start engines under water.'

'I know,' he wrote. 'Got a better idea?'

He saw Veema, like a ghost becoming corporeal, filling out into a real person, sitting at the auxiliary controls. She got up unsteadily, looking very tired, and took a few steps towards him, smiled weakly and collapsed. Instantly, he unbuckled his seat straps and staggered over to her.

Kneeling down, he cradled her head in his lap, and ran his hands through her black, curly hair. This was too real to be a dream. The last shreds of doubt fled away. He really was in a strange situation, where he couldn't speak, but there were things he could do that didn't need words. He lowered his head and kissed her long and gently on the lips. Veema's eyes opened wide and she struggled up into a sitting position, grasped him around the chest and rested her head against him. She said something softly, but he couldn't understand. He shook his head wretchedly. What he could understand was a peremptory cough behind him. Embarrassed, they unclasped each other, but neither stood up.

Camille was leaning against the control panels, in a pose he had to come to recognize. Her arms were folded across her chest, her pale fingers spread out along her black sleeves. She looked down her aquiline nose, regarding him gravely. He didn't know what to do next. They had outwitted their pursuers for now, but would his plan work?

The craft settled into the ooze at the bottom of the lake, like a tired animal at last finding solace in thick grass. It was deadly quiet. He looked towards the viewing port in the prow. At this depth, no light penetrated through the peaty water. The cold began to seep into his bones. He held Veema close to him, for his comfort as much as hers.

There was a faint tapping on the hull, then silence. All three of them froze, before looking up at the ceiling in unison. There it was again. They heard a slithering noise of something that seemed to be probing, sensing, feeling. Veema shuddered. He held her closer, and saw Camille's mouth open in horror. The noises ceased, but he felt as if he was going to suffocate. It was as if his brain had seized up. The pressure inside his skull was enormous. He closed his eyes tightly, to try to alleviate the pain.

Something rustled. Very slowly, he realised that the sound was coming from inside his head.

"Yess. You are Loratu. but you are alsso Moss."

The silky hissing words made sense to him. He felt his face taken in leathery, cool hands, and he opened his eyes and saw Veema looking at him enquiringly.

"What's the matter?" she asked.

He could hear properly at last. I have voices in my head, he thought.

He looked over to his two companions, neither of whom seemed to be affected in the same way as he was.

Where are you, he thought. He alone heard the answer, which came clearly.

"We are all around you."

"Who are you?"

There were more whispers but nothing he could interpret, until they spoke again. "We are."

"How long have you been here?"

"For ever."

"Have you spoken to any human before?"

"Only ourselvess. We did not know we could sspeak to you until now. We have lisstened for a long time. We have tried to sspeak, but you are the firsst who can hear uss."

"Where are you from?"

"Our memory iss that we come from far away in the black cold. We are everywhere in thiss world."

"I must tell the others."

"No!" It was a shout that made his head hurt viciously.

"We are ssorry to cause you pain. Do you forgive uss?"

"Yes."

"We only wisshed to be left alone."

"Wished?"

He felt himself being shaken, and he opened his eyes. Camille was kneeling in front of him.

"Are you O. K.?"

He tried to say, "Yes."

She pressed a pad and stylus into his hand. He wrote laboriously, 'It's nothing. My head hurts.'

"I'll get something for it."

"Don't take it," said the voices.

"Why not?"

"It may block our thoughtss. We cannot loose you now."

Camille put her hand on his shoulder and held a plastic cup to his mouth. He shook his head, narrowly avoiding spilling the contents. She shrugged and moved away.

"I've got to tell them."

The voices withdrew from his head. The silence was eerie, like falling into nothing. He wanted them to come back

"Will you help uss?" The voices returned with such force that he twitched involuntarily. He was dimly aware of Veema holding him and whispering something unintelligible.

"Help you. Why?"

"We are being poisoned. Our space is dying. Our home is being infected. You must stop them."

"I must see you," he thought.

Again, the silence.

★ ★ ★

Veema screamed. He looked round to see Camille kneeling on the cabin floor, staring at the view port, through which hundreds of pale, white eyes glared in at them.

"What the hell is that?" Camille whispered.

"You mean, who the hell are they?" said Moss. He was astonished; he had actually articulated, and his two companions hadn't noticed.

Camille turned a pale face to him. "Hey! you're talking sense again. Do you mean you've been in communication with *those things*?"

"Yes, I do," he said slowly.

"What do they want?" Veema mouthed at him, squeezing his arm and then burying her face in his shoulder.

He felt her shuddering breath bring moist warmth to his shirt. He hugged her tightly to him.

"I don't know," he said softly.

"But, you do." The voices in his head were insistent, crowding.

"What?"

"You help uss, we help you."

"How?" he thought. "We are in a crashed ship, at the bottom of a lake, and you want to us to help *you*?"

"We can raise your sship. Help iss on its way."

"But if you bring us to the surface, you will only alert our enemies."

"Help is on its way."

"What do you want us to do in return?"

"Help ssave our home; it is on the world circling the fourth planet from the great light you call the sun, and in return, we shall restore your memory."

★ ★ ★

"I thought you knew how to fly this thing," said Bartok.

"I do, but all this information on the inside of my helmet takes a bit of gettin' used to," Elnac grunted impatiently. "Hang on a minute. There's something comin' through; some kind of distress signal. It's very focused."

"Who's it from?"

"I dunno. I just get this feeling it's from Loratu."

"You've got this *feeling*? "said Bartok acidly. "Oh, great. Want any traps sprung, for a bit of light relief?"

"I dunno... Maybe, we ought to investigate."

"Like shit. Bet Berbek's piddling in his pants with laughter, reelin' us in."

"Nar. I don't think it's him. Not his style," said Elnac.

"Since when did 'e have *style*?" Bartok spat sideways on the floor, wiping his mouth with the back of a grimy hand.

"I say we follow it. I've plotted the co-ordinates back to Loratu's lake."

"Loratu's lake?"

"Yer. Something I saw back at base. Supposed to be very secret, but I had a little hack at the computer." said Elnac.

"Trustin' cove, ain't yer?" said Bartok.

"You gotta be, these days."

"But we sheer off at the slightest hint of trouble?"

"Of course. Don't want my arse burnt, any more than you," said Elnac, programming the navicom.

"I'm not happy about this," said Bartok

"You said. So, shut up."

"Can you put the signal on audio?" asked Bartok

Elnac flicked a switch and a steady whistling filled the cabin. As the craft flew towards it, its intensity grew.

★ ★ ★

Above the lake, Elnac halted the craft, slowly dropping down to hover above the surface. He pointed. "Look down there."

Bartok looked incredulous. "*That's* where it's coming from?"

"Yer."

"Wait a minute!" whispered Elnac. "The signal's comin' towards us."

"Well take 'er up, you fool," said Bartok.

With a whine of engines, their craft rose a short distance from the water. Below them, there was a thunderous roar as Moss's shuttle craft broke the surface of the lake. All around it the water foamed.

"Look, what's that craft down there? There's a lot of things thrashing about in the water round it," said Elnac.

"Nar, it's your imagination," said Bartok, who was watching the view screen.

They saw a hatch open in the craft below, and Loratu waving to them.

"I can't raise them ship-to-ship," said Elnac. "Their power seems to be out."

"So how did they get to the surface?"

"Blowed if I know," said Elnac.

"Don't you think we ought to lower something down to them?"

"Like what?"

"A rope ladder, or something?" Bartok said. "Aren't *you* supposed to be the brains of this outfit?"

"All right, all right. I'll go below and look."

★ ★ ★

"What's going on up there?" asked Camille.

Moss looked down at her from the hatchway.

"Someone's lowering a collapsible metal ladder."

"I hate those things."

Moss was amazed. "I thought nothing threw you."

"It's the way they sway about."

"Okay, I'll go up first, and Veema can hold on to the bottom while you go up."

"What about me, then?" said Veema, appearing out of the gloom.

"Now, don't tell me..." Moss began.

Veema laughed shortly. "Let old scaredy cat go up. See if I care."

He saw Camille give her an acidic look, but he had no time for pettiness now.

"What can we lash this end on to?"

"How about these projecting hinges?" Veema indicated the side of the hatch.

"Fine. Got a bit a wire, or something?" asked Moss.

"Don't think so. I'll look and see what I can find," said Veema, disappearing into the gloomy interior with a torch.

Moss ducked his head below the level of the hatch. The downdraft from the craft overhead was almost blinding him with spray. He looked at Camille. "Did you really mean that just now?"

"Do I have to say it twice?"

"But I..."

"You remember, I told you, back at base, I wasn't superwoman? Well," she said, lowering her eyes, "I don't like heights."

"It's not that far. I don't think they can get down any closer."

"I suppose you're right," she said in a tight voice.

"Here we are." Veema sounded just a bit too jubilant. "Tourniquet equipment. Should do beautifully. We should be up and away in no time!" She patted Camille playfully on the shoulder.

The man who said revenge is a dish best served cold was right, Moss thought.

"Aren't you forgetting something?" he said to Veema.

"What?"

"The chameleon suit."

That wiped the smile off her face.

In the event, it did not prove that difficult to make the transfer to Elnac's craft. Camille somehow steeled herself for the ascent, obviously not wanting to let herself down in front of Veema. In a fit of bravado, Veema slit the moorings on the end of the ladder, so that it dangled free as she ascended. Moss was secretly pleased that she did, as he hadn't figured out a way to release the secured end once they were all up in the other craft. But he told her off, nonetheless, for putting her life in danger. He looked down from the open hatch way as his shuttlecraft sank, bubbling into the depths. Thank you, he thought.

"Find a quiet place to lie down. We have ssomething to tell you," whispered the voices.

"What now?" Elnac asked Moss.

"Best thing is to land beside the lake and install the Chameleon suit's power pack into the ship's infrastructure, then no one can see us. You can help Veema to do it. She's done a wonderful job, so far," Moss said.

"So far?" said Veema. "Talk about damning with faint praise."

"I'm sorry. That came out all wrong. I need to have to have a lie down and think things over."

★ ★ ★

On the way back to Fort Anglesey, Berbek sat in his cabin and stared at nothing, imagining all the things he'd do to that stunt Elnac and his friend, if they ever met again. He banged one meaty fist into the other. Come on, he told himself, this was getting us nowhere. He made contact with Preston again.

"What happened?" asked Preston

"Mind you own business." Berbek waved away the question. "What's the status of the experiment?"

"We still haven't been able to trace the time stream back conclusively. It seems to have split into two. Perhaps Moss went back twice, and once was a false start, or something. It will be no problem, as long as he doesn't remember the Project. The mind block we put in place was buried deep. It wiped out twenty years of his life."

"But," said Berbek, "we still don't know why Loratu became the leader of The People of the Mist?"

"No. But his people have been very useful to blame things on, especially while they're so disorganised. The trouble will come if he ever regains his memory, and welds them back into a fighting force. As a weak leader, he has already caused disaffection. Your job, General, is supposed to be to keep it that way. Have you found him yet? We need to keep an eye on him."

"No, I haven't, but it's not your business."

"So, what are you doing about it?" Preston looked at him keenly across the miles.

"Going back to Anglesey, to interrogate various prisoners taken from his base."

"Well, you'd better make sure they talk."

"Goodbye, Bernard," Berbek said, gladly switching him off.

So, the project wasn't all that advanced. He was tired of Preston being in charge of it. The military would make far better use of it than having civilians trying to fiddle with social engineering, he thought. After all, hadn't the public returned The Party of Regeneration with a landslide majority?

They'd obviously wanted a sense of purpose, a strong leader, and not a bunch of bureaucrats in grey suits. Now they had it, in Berbek. Preston wasn't a natural leader. He was just a backroom boy with delusions of grandeur. But Britain was weak, an offshore island, with only trade links to the Eurocom combine, which was itself overawed by the tiger of the Far East. Suppose you gave the British military of the past information on the technology of the future, would it be possible to retain, or even expand, the Empire On Which the Sun Never Set?

− 8 −

Birmingham 1950

Bob Moss sat quietly in the winged armchair, hiding behind his Sunday newspaper. The clock ticked loudly on the mantelshelf. Across the sitting room sat his wife, knitting.

His face was hot. He always was afraid that, *somehow*, she could read his thoughts. Nevertheless, he couldn't help wondering what his love would be wearing today. He couldn't wait to get to the park. The clock ticked. Sunday lunch had been cleared away, the washing up done. There was nothing to stop him going out, except... He could feel the tenseness in the room. Maybe the dog felt it too. It whimpered in its sleep.

He hoped his love would be wearing his favourite things: the long dress with the buttons all the way down the front and, underneath it, the half slip and lacy white bra, and beneath the half slip, the tiny panties, and stockings held up by a minute garter belt. Sally was very slim. Everything about her was petite and beautifully formed. He felt a frisson of excitement.

They would lie together on her picnic rug, under the trees, the sun dappling through the branches, while he stroked her soft skin.

"Is anything the matter?"

He nearly jumped out of his skin. Putting down his paper, he looked innocently at his wife.

"No, dear."

"You look very red."

"It's rather stuffy in here. I think I'll go out for my walk."

His wife regarded him steadily over her half-moon spectacles, and asked, "Where are you going?"

"Just to the park, to stretch my legs."

"Well, don't be too long. You know George and Irene are coming to tea."

"Yes, dear." He'd almost forgotten those boring old farts: the wife's brother-in-law and sister. They inflicted themselves on him most Sundays. Them and their shiny new motorcar! He gritted his teeth. It was always the same. 'When are you going to earn enough to buy one like George's? Then, we can go out for a spin on Sundays in the country. You really should ask for that rise.' She hated being second-best to her sister. '*She'd* married well, hadn't she? Nice big house on that new estate…'

"And don't go out without your coat and hat, and cover up that cardigan. What will the neighbour's think?"

He would have liked to have said, "I don't care what the neighbours think."

"Won't be long," was all he managed to say. He glanced at the clock. Better get going. He was meeting Sally at three. Wouldn't have long with her today.

Getting his brown homburg hat and coat from the cloakroom, he closed the front door of their semi. The air smelt good. It wasn't far to the park, but he set off at a brisk pace, so as not to waste time.

It was five to three by the time he reached the gate-house

at the entrance to Sutton Park. He was perspiring. It was stupid to wear a coat and hat on such a day, but it was the done thing. Perhaps, one day, people would be more relaxed. As a resident of the borough, he didn't have to pay to get in, but he didn't want to be seen there. The gatekeeper might recognize him. He knew of a gap in the fence, further up the road, which gave onto an area of trees ending in heath land. He kept to the cover of a small belt of spruce, and made it across a bit of heath, which brought him into the older oak woodland without, he hoped, being observed.

He pictured Sally as he walked quickly along. At 30, she was a few years younger than him. She was only five foot three, had warm brown eyes and a pink, tip-tilted nose set in a round, smiling face. Her head was crowned with black, curly hair. She had a neat little body and the best legs he'd ever seen.

He was so lost in his thoughts that he failed to notice how the trees and light had taken on a frozen quality. It was as if the wood held its breath.

Then, something came crashing through the undergrowth towards him. It erupted from the trees, only about thirty yards away. A tall figure, clad in a silvery material, was struggling towards him in slow motion, like a deep sea diver running under water. The top of the apparition's head was flat. An oval window was built into its head-piece. In its right hand it held a black tube.

The strange being held out the tube towards him, as if with great difficulty. Bob was terrified. Hardly able to breathe, he turned and ran, instantly tripping over a log and falling headlong. He waited for the monster to fall on him, or pick him up above its head, as they do in the horror movies. But nothing happened. He risked looking round. The tube was spinning lazily towards him. It hit the grass, bounced once and settled in front of him. The figure was making a gesture to him when, in a flash of white light, it folded in on itself, flailed backwards and vanished.

He lay there, breathing deeply, trying to make sense of it all. Gradually, feeling returned to his body and sound to his surroundings. Birds began to sing again. Branches creaked in the breeze. Sally came running through the trees, her long dress billowing.

"Are you all right, my love?"

"Yes, I think so." He turned over. Nothing was hurting.

"Something very strange just happened," she said. "It was if someone turned the sound off in the wood and then there was this whooshing noise… and… and… Are you sure you're OK?"

"Yes, I'm OK," he said, getting up and knocking the soil off his coat.

"You look as if you've seen a ghost. Come and lie down with me."

He decided not to tell her about the strange figure. She'd think he was mad. He picked up the tube. His fingers froze round it, claw like.

"Ow! *My hand!*"

She knelt down and took his icy hand between her small, warm ones. Warmth seeped back into him.

"How did you do that?" he asked, amazed.

"I don't know," she said faintly. "It just seemed the right thing to do."

"My hand feels better already."

"What is that tube thing?"

"Don't know." He took a deep breath. "I just I tripped

up, when I was going forward to get it."

She looked at him. She doesn't believe me, he thought.

"Come and sit on our rug and we'll have a look at it together."

"Right," he said, staggering to his feet, still holding the tube, which tingled to his touch.

"Aren't you pleased to see me?"

"Of course I am." He gave a faint smile.

"You don't look it"

"I'll be all right in a minute."

She reached up, put her arms around his neck and kissed him full on the mouth. He put one arm round her slender waist and returned her kiss. They stood holding each other for a long time, her head on his chest. Eventually, she looked up at him and smiled.

"Better now?"

"Yes, much." He didn't feel it. He grasped her hand. "Let's go and sit down," he said, leading her through the trees.

A rug was laid out under their usual tree, and a flask of tea and some biscuits stood ready.

"Let's have some tea, and you can tell me all about it!"

She ran ahead and sat down gracefully, tucking her skirt neatly round her legs. The pearl buttons down the front of her dress glistened in the sunshine. She looked good enough to eat. He sat down heavily, passing a hand over his forehead.

"Are you sure you didn't hurt yourself?" Her smile changed to a look of concern.

"No, it's nothing, just a slight headache."

"Have some tea. That'll perk you up," she said, pulling the cork from the neck of the thermos flask. She filled two plastic cups with tea.

He picked up the tube. It was now the same temperature

as the surrounding air. It didn't look much, just black and the same size as Sally's thermos, but quite heavy. It was sealed with flat disks at both ends. There didn't seem any way to open it. He shook it close to his ear, but he could hear nothing.

"Here, let me look," she said, holding out her hands.

"But it might be a bomb!"

"Don't be silly," she said with assurance, taking it firmly from him.

She tried twisting it at both ends and pulling at it. No crack showed in the matt black casing.

"I'm going to have my tea, before it gets cold," she said, handing it back to him.

In his turn, he tried unscrewing and pulling at it, but he couldn't get it open either. He put it down. With a faint click, a silver dot appeared at one end, and then he noticed a line in gold rotating round the circumference, three inches from one end. They waited to see if anything else would happen, but nothing did.

"I think this thing is meant for you," she said, laying a hand on his arm, "Go on, open it!"

He found that it was very stiff, but made no sound when he unscrewed the end and pulled it off.

Inside, he could see the charred end of a roll of papers. Gently, he pulled them out and read the top one, holding his breath.

"I don't believe it!"

"What's the matter?" she said, craning forward.

"Someone knows about us, Sally," he whispered.

– 9 –

Birmingham 2010

Bill Patterson never liked these jobs; going through the house of someone recently deceased, poking into the remnants of a life. This time, it held a special poignancy for him. He remembered this particular client with affection. Dear old Sally. Always polite. Always paid her bills promptly. You could see, even at ninety, that she had been beautiful once.

He inserted the key in the front door of the little terraced house, and let Fred Stableford, the valuer, enter first. Their breath steamed in the winter air. It was as cold inside as it was out.

"Doesn't this ever get you down, Fred?" Bill asked, rubbing his hands together to warm them.

Fred Stableford sniffed the stuffiness of the front room. "You get used to it, just like you do with those messy divorces."

"Oh, no, I never get used to them, especially the endless fighting over trivia. Where shall we start?"

"At the top and work down. Where's your usual probate girl?"

"On holiday," Bill said, thinking of all that extra work waiting for him back at the office.

"So, I'm stuck with you, then."

Bill attempted a laugh. "If I'd known, I'd have worn a blond wig."

"You could have sent someone else."

Bill paused for a moment and then said quietly, "This client was special. Sort of unfinished business, if you like."

Bill led the way through into the back room and opened the door onto the steep, dark stairs.

"It's amazing she ever got up these." Fred said.

Bill thought of his last visit. She'd been so alive, when she waved him off from the front steps. Never thought I wouldn't see her again, he thought. "I think she lived her last years downstairs. Bathroom and loo are out the back. You go up first, Fred. I'll take my time."

"O.K." said Fred, disappearing into the gloom.

Bill hauled himself up the stairs, using the handrail, cursing his artificial hip, and groaning inwardly at the pain. Why put himself through this? He *could've* sent someone else, except for that note in the will.

Fred was in the front bedroom. "Your hip acting up again?" He asked.

"It won't kill me. Let's get on."

Bill watched as his friend methodically worked his way around the room. He saw him pick up a candlestick from the dressing table. "What about this?"

"Black Wedgwood. Worthless."

Bill felt sad. No doubt it had been a treasured object.

Fred looked up from his clipboard. "Right. Now for the back."

They crossed the narrow hall at the top of the stairs and went into the back bedroom.

"Look, I know you. Is this something more than a valuation exercise, Bill? Are we looking for something in particular?" asked Fred.

"Yes, as a matter of fact, that is exactly right."

Bill sat down on the faded counterpane of the narrow bed, and scratched his greying beard. I wonder whether I should tell Fred the whole story. After all, he is an old friend, he thought.

"Look," he said hesitantly, "you must keep this to yourself, OK?"

Fred nodded.

"She was very particular. Not the sort of person given to flights of fancy..."

"Yes, and...?"

"It was after she left her cohabitee, Robert Moss. She was planning to marry someone called Fairin, when she came to me for some advice about her will. It was when she..."

"Go on."

"She was carrying on about men's secretiveness. Then, she suddenly started telling me about something that happened years back, in Sutton Park. Bob Moss had found this black cylinder. It had contained some papers, according to what he told her, but she never saw them properly. The contents had bothered him so much that, in the end, he'd had the cylinder welded shut, so no one could get into it. For some strange reason, on his last access visit to their child Arthur, he gave her the cylinder and made her promise to keep it safe. Then he'd been killed in a road accident. She said it was almost as if he *knew* he was going to die. Well, she outlived Fairin, her husband. They had only had the one child, John, but she didn't trust him, for some reason. She wanted me to dispose of the cylinder permanently, after she was dead."

Fred sat down on the bed beside him. "That's a lot to take in at one go."

I think I've said far too much, thought Bill. It's not like me to go blabbing on. Fred sat looking at the floor.

"And where is this mysterious thing?"

"She told me it's walled up in the kitchen."

"Well, why didn't you say so?" said Fred.

"I don't know." But, I do know, thought Bill.

"I *was* going to look for it on my own but I had second thoughts. As I wasn't sure exactly what I was going to find, I thought I'd better have a witness."

Fred clapped him on the shoulder and said, "You're a strange man. Did you bring a hammer and chisel?"

Bill nodded. "Of course I did. They're still in the car."

"Right then! Let's get at it!"

They descended the creaking stairs and went into the back kitchen. Fred's shoes scrunched on the linoleum. He looked down. In the wall was the papered-over the bulge of the backroom chimney, and there, about four feet from the floor, where the fireplace used to be, was a large, ragged hole.

"Oh... bugger!" said Fred, quietly. "Someone's beaten us to it. That's dropped you in the 'proverbial'."

Bill leant against the door frame. "You can say that again."

★ ★ ★

"It's jus' rubbish. Trash. All that trouble we went to. For nothing." In disgust, Terry Hackett threw the canister down on the oil-sodden garage floor. "You *said* she'd got sparklers hidden in that house, and there's only bloody papers in this tin."

His brother, Shane, raised the visor from his grubby face and turned off the oxy-acetylene torch.

"Well, me information was good. Joey said he'd been in the house to do some building work, and when he replaced the bricks covering the old lady's fireplace, he saw this tin in the grate. He said it had to hold something worth nicking. He couldn't very well walk off with it, not with the old girl breathing down his neck and offering him cups of tea, could he?"

"Joey the Greek? Oh, pull the other one! That man's bonkers. He's got far too much imagination. Sparklers, in a rotten old tin! You ought to have had more sense than to listen to him."

"You went along with it."

"More fool me," said Terry.

"What we do now, then?" Shane took off his heavy gloves and dropped them on the chipped workbench.

"Get rid of it. I never want to see it again."

"Where shall we dump it, then?"

Terry looked round the small lock-up garage.

"Certainly not here, and don't leave it in the bin, our Shane. Fuzz'll trace us, easy as breathing"

"I'll take it to the dump, shall I?"

"Oh, do what you bloody like, but do it now."

Shane picked up the cylinder and regarded it bitterly. "All right. All right. Perfect bloody end to a bloody awful day."

★ ★ ★

Liberty knew he shouldn't be here. His mum would be furious. "You'll catch something, messing around that dump," she'd say, but he was Long John Silver and it was Treasure Island. He got it from an old book of his dad's. His mum threw out all the stuff that dad hadn't taken with him, but the boy had managed to retrieve the book, just before the men came to empty the wheelie bin that served their tiny flat.

He looked across the ranks of low-rise buildings that were crammed onto the estate, all in the same yellow brick, with red pitched roofs. It was difficult to tell from here, on the dump, which of them was his home. An elevated section of road rose like a great snake, curving off into the distance beyond the houses. The roar of traffic was ever-present. An aircraft whined overhead as it was coming into land at Birmingham International airport.

He'd squeezed through a gap in the fence. Just yesterday, they'd started to bulldoze the dump site, to make room for more houses. Seagulls screeched and fought over old vegetable peelings. Great gouges in the earth around his island had filled with rainwater. That was the sea, or what he imagined it would look like.

He wore an old, brown raincoat of his father's, one sleeve pinned up. He limped about, making Ooo-Arr noises and leaning heavily on a stick. He'd tried using it as a crutch, just like the real Long John Silver, but it was too long and he didn't have the strength to break it.

From behind him came scrambling noises. Micky Buckle, the big kid from Cornwall Road, came clambering over a pile of old mattresses and bits of sodden fibreboard.

"What're you doing 'ere? I told you not to come 'ere no more. This is my patch."

"Sorry, Micky."

"I'll make you sorry, Moss. Come 'ere"

Micky, in his filthy T-shirt and baggy trousers cut off below the knee, loomed over him. Liberty didn't move.

"I said come 'ere, you little tyke."

What was it his mother always said? "You've got to stand

up to these bullies."

Micky advanced. Liberty tensed and, just when the other boy was in range, he lashed out with his stick. It landed heavily against the side of the bully's flabby stomach.

"You little bastard! I'll get you for that!"

Micky launched himself across the decaying sludge and grabbed Liberty round the middle. Together, they rolled over and over, until the bigger boy was on top and Liberty's face was pressed into the mud.

"Surrender?"

"Goh," he gurgled, unable to speak.

Micky wrenched Liberty's arm up his back.

"Hey, you there!" a rough male voice shouted.

Micky let go of Liberty, who craned his head round and saw a large man, in a yellow helmet and jacket, jumping over mounds of rubbish towards them.

"What's going on?" The man said.

"Nothin'," said Micky sourly.

"Let the kid go."

Micky didn't move

"I *said,* let the kid go, or you'll get some of your own back."

"He was interfering."

"With what? Clear off, the pair of you. This place is off-limits. You could get hit by machinery, or something. Go on, bugger off."

The two boys staggered to their feet.

"I'd better not see you again," said Micky.

Liberty, greatly daring, stuck his tongue out.

"Oh, just get out of here," said the man impatiently.

They shambled off in different directions. Liberty went to look for his gap in the fence, but the workmen had already found it and closed it up. He had to go out through the main gate, past a group of men in muddy, fluorescent yellow overalls, drinking tea and smoking by the hut. They scarcely looked at him. His island was gone. It would never be the same again.

When he got home, of course, his mother was terribly angry. He was filthy and his sweat shirt was torn.

"Where are we going get another one, then? We're not made of money, you know."

"Sorry, mum."

"You will be. Go to bed now, without any supper, and you'll stay in after school for a week. No, make that two weeks. Go on, get out of my sight, you little wretch."

He sat down heavily on his bed. At least he had his treasure. He'd found it sometime ago, quite by chance, when he was scavenging there with the other boys. It gave him a very strange feeling, almost as if someone was calling to him. It sent a cold shudder shooting up his spine. He'd come running up a spoil heap, tripped and fallen head over heels down the other side. He'd sat up, nursing his cut knee. He was worried about getting about lockjaw. His friend, Wayne, said they couldn't get your teeth apart, and you starved to death, or they had to break your teeth, which left you in a horrible bloody mess, and they had to feed you through a straw.

And there it was. He hadn't seen it at first. Then, the sun had come out, and he saw it lying in a puddle of water, as if it had rolled out of some other rubbish and down the slope. A black canister. Like his mum's thermos, but without the handle. And *really* black. Light sort of fell into it. He'd reached forward and picked it up. A ring of rust had formed round it where one end must have been unscrewed, and it was silvery in places, as if it had been opened quite recently. He'd tried to twist it open, but it was too difficult.

He'd heard someone shout behind him, "Oi, what you got there?"

He'd turned. Another boy had been sliding down the heap towards him.

"Nothing." He'd hastily stuffed it into his canvas shoulder bag.

"Oh, give us a look!"

But he'd been off, running, leaving the boy standing there. Breathing hard, he'd got to the gap in the fence and squeezed through.

He'd been a bit disappointed with the treasure, when he got it home. His mum was out, which was why he'd managed to go out on his own. He'd flopped down on the bed and tried once more to open it. After a bit of effort, the tube seemed suddenly to respond to him, as if by magic. He could feel warmth under his fingers. But, instead of treasure, it was full of old papers, charred at one end and very damp. They weren't particularly interesting; about people he didn't know, and stuff about DNA. He'd asked the teacher about DNA, the next day, at school, but she'd reacted very strangely, and he'd had to stay in at home-time and write out a hundred times, "I must not ask silly questions."

Anyway, it was his and nobody else's. It might be valuable. Code messages from a spy that had got lost, or, perhaps, he'd got murdered and couldn't get back for them. They'd be looking all over for them, those men in black suits and dark glasses. He'd better just check it was still there. He opened his wardrobe and dug into the back, under the smelly old trainers and stuff he'd rescued from the rubbish dump, and lifted up the bit of loose board he'd long ago prised off.

The treasure was gone.

They'd found it. The men in black. He imagined them in the hall, whispering to his mum. He was so engrossed that he didn't hear the front door open and his mother come up the corridor and into his bedroom. When she spoke, it made his heart jump.

"This place is a *tip*. And don't think I don't know about your secret place in the wardrobe. What you wanted with them old papers and all that other trash, I don't know. I've thrown it all away. And if I ever catch you going to that tip again and bringing rubbish home, it'll be no dinner for a week. Do you understand?"

She banged the door shut, and he heard her shuffling down the corridor in her loose slippers, slamming the kitchen door. He got into bed, pulled the duvet up over his head, and wept.

He dreamt uneasily. His treasure was calling to him. It was lying out on the tip, under the moon, humming. But how was he to get out? He couldn't cling to the wall outside his bedroom window, like they do in the comics. He was three storeys up. But he had a key. He would just have to wait until his mother was asleep.

It was a long wait. At last, about midnight, he heard his mother flush the toilet and close her bedroom door, and all was quiet. He waited another ten minutes, just to make sure, then he got out of bed, already wearing his tee shirt and trousers. Carrying his trainers, and knowing which boards creaked, he tiptoed down the corridor to the front door. The lock squeaked loudly in the stillness, but nothing disturbed his mother's snoring.

He stepped out onto the cold concrete of the walkway outside and quietly pulled the door shut behind him, hardly daring to breathe. It wasn't until he had got to the bottom of the last flight of stairs that he paused for a moment and put on his trainers.

Outside, there were very few street lights on, because of the power cuts; even so, the sky was never fully dark. At night, it took on a nasty, fuzzy orange colour. It was all to do with England being cut off from Europe, and Europe having trouble with the Tiger people. He didn't really understand all that.

There was no one about. There wouldn't be any police. They never went anywhere, except in cars, and very fast, as if they were afraid. The dump was outlined against the orange sky. He found a place where the earth was loose, and squirmed under the fence. He stood up, listening. In the background, was the roar of traffic. It never seemed to get quieter, even with the petrol shortage he'd heard about.

At night, the dump had a threatening, alien look. He was half thinking of going back, when he saw something white flash between the heaps to his right. Cautiously, he moved towards them, and then dropped flat as a torch beam swept in his direction.

"Anything, Don?"

"No. Just your imagination. Let's get back to the hut and have a brew." The two security guards went off towards the main gates.

The air was very cool and still, as if it were holding its breath. He thought he could hear, and then felt, a hum that started in the ground and spread through his whole body. With difficulty, he raised his head over the lip of the mound. For a moment, he could see nothing, then a hot wind blew towards him and out of the air stepped a spaceman. His suit glowed white against the black heaps. He had a flat head, and monstrous arms and legs that moved in slow motion.

The spaceman was looking for something, his feet scraping the rubble. Then, he looked up. Liberty ducked down. He could hear the spaceman coming towards him. The boy put his hands together and prayed hard.

"I promise I'll be very good," he whispered. "Please don't let him get me. Please. I shouldn't have taken it."

Liberty just had to have another look. He raised his head again, just in time to see the spaceman pick up something cylindrical and dark. It showed up against the glow of his space suit. Then, the spaceman appeared to fold up into himself, and, with a soundless flash of white light, he was gone.

Liberty shivered convulsively. Then he saw torches coming towards him and heard voices. He'd better get out quick. It was a long, cold walk home, and when he got there his mum was waiting.

– 10 –

Life Streams

Moss closed the door of his tiny cabin and lay back on the narrow bunk, recessed into the wall. Now that the chameleon circuits had been installed and tested, he had given orders for Elnac to fly the craft to Base 2, under the dunes on the Dovey estuary, in mid Wales. That would have to do, while he thought about regrouping. As soon as he lay down, the voices were back.

"Are you ready to concentrate?"

"As ready as I'll ever be."

It was not a pleasant experience. He was falling backwards through thick white smoke that gradually changed to a grey twilight. The silence was suffocating. He started to thrash about. "Let me out! Let me out!"

"Patience. Clear your mind. Be calm."

Gradually, he drifted downwards, leaning back. He found that he was standing. He moved his feet. It was firm underfoot. A dark, humanoid figure appeared, walking towards him.

"Hello, son."

Moss looked into a face lit from below with a soft yellow light. "Dad? Dad? It can't be you. You're…"

Moss knew at once that it was his father. He saw again the long, narrow face, bushy eyebrows and the deep-set, brown eyes. The voice, too, was unchanged.

"Not now, son. I've got so much to tell you. Do you remember Project Alpha?"

"No. So much of my past life is a blank."

"I will help you remember." His father stretched out his hand and grasped Moss's unresisting fingers. The touch was cool, but not unpleasant. "Come with me. There's nothing to fear."

Together, they walked steadily forwards. The twilight brightened, and a scene, at first translucent, solidified round them. Moss saw that they were standing in a laboratory. Men in white coats were working on equipment arranged on battered brown tables scarred with chemical residue.

"Can they hear us?"

"No. We are not really here. We are reconstructing from a different angle what you have already seen."

"Are you saying, you can give me back my memories! But…"

"Quiet now, and watch."

Moss peered forward and gripped his father's hand even more tightly. "That's… that's me over there!"

"Yes. Watch and learn."

"Who is that?"

"Professor Krabowitz. Can you see his security pass on his coat?"

"What are they doing?"

"Recreating Gunter Nimtz's experiment with music and time. Stop asking questions. Just watch."

Moss could hear Mozart's fortieth symphony. Suddenly, it speeded up, until it became a screech, just on the edge of hearing. It was being fed into a coder that broke it down into binary, and then fed it into a photon generator. Somehow, he remembered seeing this before. The signal from a decoder, a short distance away, emerged as a perfectly recognizable melody. What Krabowitz was doing should be impossible. Quantum tunnelling allowed occasional random photons to break the light-speed barrier, but it should be impossible to transmit information faster than light – but the music was information, wasn't it?

He felt a tug on his hand. "Come this way."

They walked through the technicians as if they did not exist, and on into daylight. From it came an echoing voice.

"Everyone says physics puts a limit on how far back a time traveller can travel. Relativity theory says, in general, once you've made a time machine, you can't go back to the period of time before it was made."

Moss found himself standing high above rank upon rank of sitting people in a raked lecture theatre. On a dais below, a small wiry man with wild, white hair and thick glasses was standing in front of a screen. The very picture of a mad scientist. What he was saying was, however, anything but mad.

"Along came the Holy Grail of quantum gravity. The hard evidence for parallel universes has been around ever since 1909, with the Young Slit Interference Pattern experiment. So it is possible, ladies and gentlemen, to send information back through time." The audience rose as one, applauded and stamped their feet. There was sporadic whistling. The lecturer appealed for silence, by holding his hands palm down and lowering them. Eventually, the audience sat down.

"Any questions? You, sir, at the back?"

A young man stood up.

Moss gasped. "That's me again!"

"Professor Chow says that, to have a genuine signal, you

really have to *control* the signal. But in quantum mechanical tunnelling, it's a completely random process. He says you cannot send information with the tunnelling particle."

"Young man, have you not been paying attention? You saw on the video, that we sent the Mozart 40 at 4.7 times the velocity of light, over a distance of 14 centimetres. Did you not recognize the piece of music received at the other end? Despite the random nature of the process, the Mozart came through recognisably. You heard it, didn't you? Remember Young's experiment. Two photons, on their own, couldn't make the ripple effect. That means there was *another* photon, in a parallel course, that we couldn't see, acting on the photons in our universe to make them change direction. That's why it's possible to send information back through time. Going faster than light, the message goes backwards in time, but not in a random fashion."

His father whispered in his ear, "Come with me. I've got one last thing to show you."

They turned away from the lecture theatre and passed through the wall. In a flash of light that stung Moss's sight, there came a voice that was oddly familiar, yet Moss could not remember whose it was. They emerged onto a gantry, overlooking a cavernous hall hewn out of rock.

"Where are we?"

"In one of the underground caves in Guernsey dug out by the Nazis in World War Two."

"Who's that?" Moss pointed to a tall, gaunt man with steel-rimmed spectacles.

"That's Bernard Preston, the man who stole your memory. He has continued Goldmann's experiments, using huge sums of secret government money. He has succeeded in sending inanimate objects back through time. You forged a pass and got into his laboratory. You have been back in time, three times. You took a hell of a risk. On the first two occasions, you overshot and saw your grandfather, and then, yourself at 10 years old. On the third occasion, you managed to leave a message with yourself at twenty. But after that, they began to take an interest in you. Eventually, you were arrested, but you escaped. What you really wanted to do was slow up the discovery of DNA, so that the consequent discoveries that have wrecked your world couldn't happen, or not until mankind had grown up enough to behave in a different way. You kept going, looking for answers, until they got you again, just recently, when Preston's medics used his experimental probe on you. If it hadn't been for the bravery of your friends, you'd be there still."

"But how could I do it, if all Preston's people had managed to do was send inanimate objects?"

"We don't know how you did it. That information has been erased from your brain. Somehow, you got information from the future that enabled you to travel in a protective suit, albeit very briefly. It was long enough to leave information behind."

"What must I do to get my memory back, Dad?"

"We are not your father. You can call us the Asgathi. We are using your father's image as a more convenient way of focusing your thoughts. We will restore your memory, by breaking the scar tissue caused by those crude experiments, if you do something for us in return. Stop them sending the probe to Europa. It has not been decontaminated properly. That was considered too expensive, and not worth the effort, and you humans assume that nothing lives on Europa, anyway. The arrogance of you people. You indiscriminately send your germs out into space, with no thought for their impact on any other life-forms."

"I'm sure our space scientists don't realise what they're doing. I don't see how I can help you, though."

"You will. The more investigations we make, the clearer it will become. We have already enabled you to speak again. Do we have an agreement about you helping uss? The work you are doing now may provide the answer to how you can help uss."

"I agree."

"Very well. We shall now return you to consciousness. We shall be listening and watching. One thing more, and this will influence everything, Preston plans to kill Veema by murdering her grandmother."

His father turned to go.

"Come back, dad. There is so much I must ask you."

"No. We have said enough. Goodbye."

Moss felt totally disorientated. Far off, as if it was happening to someone else, he felt himself coughing violently and gasping for air. The pain in his head was terrible. He was brought back to consciousness of his surroundings by the sound of furious knocking on the cabin door.

"Are you all right?"

Veema's voice. "I heard you cry out."

"I'm O.K."

"Let me in. I want to see you."

He didn't want her to see him like this. He got up unsteadily and lurched over to the washbasin, threw some water over his face, and gave it a quick wipe with a disposable towel from the dispenser. He unlocked the door and pulled it open a crack.

"Is there anybody with you?"

"No. You look awful. What's up?"

He let her in.

"The Asgathi gave me a bad time."

"The who?"

"Those gestalt beings in the lake."

"They're still in contact with you?" She looked concerned.

"They seem to be getting more and more powerful by the minute."

"What do they want of you?"

"What's your surname?" He asked, not really needing to know the answer. He knew it already.

"Price. Why?"

"It's not really Price," he said.

"Whatever to you mean?"

"It's Fairin. You changed it to Price, in honour of your grandmother."

"She was a wonderful woman... but..."

Revelation struck him. "So that's how it's done!"

"You're not making much sense." There was a hard edge to her voice.

"You're the girl in the newsreel, aren't you? I remember your placard: NATURAL SELECTION – NATURAL BIRTH."

"How the hell do you know that?"

She sat down heavily on the bunk next to him.

"The Lady in Bl..., Camille showed me a vid, back at the base, when I was recovering. You were on it. I paused the picture, wishing I knew you."

"But, you do know me. From the first time we met, I fell in love with you and you with me. You saved me from the Sterilisers, for God's sake! Don't you remember that, even?"

It all came out in a rush, and she started to cry bitterly, her hands clasped tight together, her head bowed. "And now you don't remember me at all!"

"I wish I could. Oh, how I wish I could," he said, staring in front of him.

"Then, let me help you." She put her arms round his shoulders, gently turning him towards her, but he turned his face away.

"I can't afford to get close to you again," he said, his voice breaking. "If you were taken from me, I couldn't bear it."

"Nobody's going to do that, I promise you," she said softly.

"No. You don't understand... Preston's going to murder you."

"Oh that! I've lived with *that* for years, so what else is new?"

"It's the way he's going to do it."

"What do you mean?"

"He's going to murder Sally Fairin, your paternal grandmother."

"Don't be ridiculous!" She was angry now. "How could he murder her? She's been dead for years. What are you up to?"

"That's what the Asgathi told me."

She calmed down a bit. "I see," she said, tightly. "And you believe them? They've got their own motives for telling you things like that, you know."

"How can you possibly know about their motives? It's me they talk to."

"Nothing's for nothing in this world, or theirs! What have they made you promise?"

He brushed her question aside. "So, we're going to

Guernsey."

"Guernsey? What do we want to put our heads in the lion's mouth for?"

"It's where Preston is conducting his experiments into time."

"How are you going to stop Sally being murdered?"

"They're going to join my mind to the mind of whoever Preston sends to murder her."

"Oh." She was absorbed in thought for a moment, looking at the floor. "You mean one minute, I might be here... and the next minute...?"

"Yes. That's why I've got to stop him."

"*We've* got to stop him." She perked up. "Well, if I could go any minute, we'd better make the most of it." She pulled his head round and her mouth was on his, hungrily. He closed his eyes, determined to remember every last moment. Her tongue entered his mouth. He didn't need to remember what to do next.

As he came into the cockpit, Moss saw Elnac look up from the navicom.

"Change course."

"What? Where we goin', then?"

"Guernsey."

Bartok half rose from the other seat and looked round at Moss. "You out of your mind?"

"No, he's not," said Veema, coming through the door.

Bartok leered at her. "You two had a good time, then?"

Her face hardened. He stopped smiling and turned away.

Moss looked around the cockpit and asked, "Where's Camille?"

"She's gone off to her cabin," said Elnac. "She didn't look too good."

"That's not like her," said Veema. "I'll go and see how she's doing."

"Why are we going to Guernsey?" asked Bartok.

"That's where they're doing the experiments," Moss explained.

Elnac swivelled his chair round to face him "On what?"

"Time."

"Come again?" said Bartok.

"If they succeed, none of us will exist."

Elnac sucked his teeth. "Seems as good a reason as any. Guernsey it is, then. You're the boss."

"You got a plan?" Bartok was not to be put off.

"Yes, I've got a plan," said Moss, grinning. He turned at the sound of running footsteps on metal. Veema hurled herself through the hatchway.

"Can't find her!"

"Bloody hell!" roared Bartok.

"Right, you and Elnac take the forward cabins. Veema, you're with me," said Moss, pushing past her and out into the corridor.

They found Camille slumped in a small storeroom. She was white and shivering.

"What do you think's wrong with her?" he asked Veema.

Veema grasped Camille's wrist and looked at it. "She's having a bad trip."

"Why should she do such a thing?"

"You tell me."

Camille looked up at him in a dazed, pleading way, but there was no light in her eyes.

"Let's get you back to your cabin," he said.

He and Veema lugged Camille along the corridor, each holding her under one armpit, and lifted her onto her bunk. Veema covered her with a blanket.

"I'm going to sit with her," she said.

"OK. Call me if her condition changes."

Bartok was lounging against the outside of the cockpit entrance. "How is she?"

"Difficult to say. She's shivering a lot."

"It's not drugs, is it?" Bartok suggested.

"Do you know anything about this?"

"Not me. Any road, she's so darned secretive."

"What made you ask that, if you don't know anything about her using drugs?"

"She must be on something; how else can she keep going without any sleep?" Bartok said.

"Veema's keeping an eye on her. We don't know what's wrong with her yet," he told Bartok. Moss ducked into the cockpit and asked Elnac, "What's our E.T.A.?"

"One hour and eighteen minutes," said Elnac, "Where exactly are they doing these experiments?"

"In some old caves, dug out by the Nazis in the Second World War."

Elnac whistled. "That's a long time ago."

"What's Nazis?" asked Bartok.

"A military dictatorship."

"What happened to them in the end?" Bartok continued.

"It's a long story." Moss said with a sigh.

Bartok grinned. "So, you reckon we can just walk into one of the most heavily guarded places in England and say 'Hello! We just happen to be passing', do you?"

"They've got acoustic nets, brilliant mines, underwater cameras, and that's just in the sea," said Elnac.

"How come you know so much?" asked Moss.

Elnac chuckled. "I didn't tell you about that little job, did I?"

"But most of their defences are no good without power," said Moss. "You and Bartok are going to knock out their generator. It's independent of the town, and sited close to the sea. That's where the coolant water comes from."

Elnac looked at him dubiously. "How'd you know all this about their defences?"

"Veema established the first cell of the People on the island. The generators are a bit antiquated, and need plenty of air, so the intakes are outside, in a cleft of the hillside. Veema's downloaded some schematics."

He put a pad in front of them and pointed to the diagram of the electrical layout. "It's not guarded very well, for some reason. You'll have to knock out the relays first. They take electricity into the complex. Don't blow everything up, or we'll never get inside."

He turned when Veema came in through the door, and asked, "How is she?"

"I think you ought to take a look at her."

★ ★ ★

Camille was lying under a blanket and shivering. Her face was paler than usual, but she was conscious. Moss lowered himself onto the end of the bunk, on a level with Veema, who sat on a chair by Camille's head.

"Have you ever seen anything like this before?" he asked.

"It looks to me as if she's suffering from withdrawal

symptoms."

Camille whispered something. He lent to close to hear. She lifted her head painfully of the pillow. "Tell her to piss off," she whispered.

"What did she say?" asked Veema.

"I think she wants you to go."

Veema scowled. "All right. See you later."

The door closed and he heard her footsteps fade down the corridor. Camille raised herself with difficulty onto one elbow. Her voice was husky and quiet.

"Unlucky in love? Why worry? With a little practice, you can be unlucky at cards too."

"What have you done to yourself?"

"Why should you care?"

"I care."

"She goes and gets herself captured, through inexperience, and nearly gets us all killed into the bargain, and I have to hold it all together. Now you're restored to us, you don't remember the prize mess she made of everything. You don't remember me, either, do you?" She lay back exhausted. Moss took her hand, but she pulled it away with an effort. Tears trickled from the corners of her eyes. He got up to go, feeling inadequate to cope with her in her present condition. At the door, he paused.

"Camille, I wish I could help you. I don't understand what's wrong, but if I *can* help, please tell me."

"I don't want you to go to Guernsey." She was barely audible.

"We've got to. You must stay here and get better. Can I get you anything for the pain?"

"You're not the same person you used to be, Loratu."

"I don't know the person I used to be," he replied sadly.

She tried to sit up again. "Promise me one thing before you go. Kill the bastard that did this to me."

"You mean Preston?"

She nodded dumbly. Then she said, so quietly that he could barely hear, "Do you know about project Alpha?"

"Tell me what *you* know, Camille. Let's see."

"Experiments with time. On Guernsey. Preston's going to… terminate you."

"How?"

"I don't know. It's something to do with the Alpha experiment."

"How do you know?" he asked, but she just waved a hand wearily.

"Well, we're going, and that's that. Rest now and I'll look in on you later."

She closed her eyes. Was there the suspicion of a smile there? He closed the door quietly behind him and walked back to the cockpit.

"Okay, you lot," he said, entering the cabin. "Let's get this show on the road."

★ ★ ★

"Well?" said Preston, looking up. "What do you think? Will he come?"

Preston's head of security turned away from the screen. "I don't think so."

"Oh, he'll come, all right. You don't know my Camille."

– 11 –

Into the Time Tunnels

Preston was in his private office, and he looked up petulantly from his work, when the intercom buzzed.

He sighed and activated the screen in front of him.

"Yes, what is it? I told you I wasn't to be interrupted."

His chief security officer's face appeared on screen.

"There's been peculiar interference on all frequencies, in and out. We can't decode anything yet."

"Is that all?" Preston's finger was poised to cut him off.

"Yes... No. Perimeter screens just snapped on, sir."

"So our man is here at last, is he?"

"Not him, exactly."

The colour drained from the security officer's cheeks. The screen momentarily went blank. The dark countenance of Garvie Berbek appeared next.

"Expecting someone else, were we?" Berbek asked.

Preston pretended to be unperturbed. "What can I do for you, Garvie?"

"I've come to see what you're spending all that money on. Open the landing bay doors."

"And, if I refuse?"

"I'll have great pleasure in blowing them off." Momentarily, his face was replaced on the screen by the image of a sky filled with black, wedge-shaped cruisers. "See what I mean?"

* * *

"Shit!" cursed Elnac, clapping a hand to the side of his helmet.

Moss looked up from his pad. "What is it?"

"Berbek's landed on Guernsey, and he don't sound too pleased, neither."

"Do you know how many ships are involved?" Moss asked.

"However many there are, they're going to be too much for us," said Veema, shaking her head ruefully.

"Veer off, Elnac, and make it fast," said Moss.

The craft instantly shot sideways and upwards, streaking away from Guernsey at full speed.

"What do we do now?" growled Bartok.

"Quiet, everyone." said Elnac, still clutching his helmet. "Berbek's asking Preston to surrender the Guernsey base to him."

"Surrender? What the hell!" Moss exclaimed.

"He wants the whole experiment turned over to him."

"We'd better make ourselves scarce," said Veema.

Moss nodded. "My thoughts exactly." He tapped something out on the memory board and handed it to Elnac. "Feed these co-ordinates into the navicom."

"Where we goin'?" Elnac asked.

"To the Jubilee Bunker," said Moss.

"What's going on?" Camille had appeared, and was leaning in at the cockpit door. She looked pale and sickly, but was on her feet.

Veema gasped. "You know what's going on, don't you, Camille?"

"I don't know what you mean!" But the shock on Camille's face was plain to see. She staggered away from the doorway and disappeared.

Moss turned to Veema. "Have we got any agents in Preston's base?"

"Not that I know of."

"Elnac, do a narrow-band, internal sweep of this craft," Moss said.

"Done it. Nothing there, boss."

"Well, tighten the sweep and try again."

"I got something, this time," Elnac said, grinning in satisfaction.

"Where's it coming from?"

"Three guesses."

Veema started to move. "I think it's time I had another look at Camille, don't you?"

Moss grabbed her by the arm and shook his head. Then he went over to Elnac and whispered something in his ear. Elnac grunted.

"What's he want?" Bartok asked Elnac.

Elnac, busy at the controls, ignored him. He gave Moss the thumbs-up sign. Moss turned to go out of the cockpit.

Veema stopped him and looked questioningly at him. She was about to say something, when Moss gestured for her to follow him and led her from the room. Once they were out in the corridor, he pulled her to him and whispered in her ear.

"We don't know what kind of bug she's put in the cockpit. I'm banking on her not having one out here."

"How did you know?" She whispered back.

"She must have bugged my cabin. From something Elnac told me, I'd say she disappeared, looking ill, at around the time I told you I was going to Guernsey. She must have told Preston we were going there. Her plan was to stay out of the way, I think. Anyway, she was originally intending to persuade me to go there herself. She can't have known what the Asgathi were going to tell me. The fact that Berbek's now shown up has really shaken her."

As quietly as possible, they crept down the corridor to Camille's cabin. Moss pressed the door-stud and the door slid open. All they could see was a rumpled blanket on the bunk. Veema turned to look at Moss. Camille was gone.

A black figure lunged from the left, grabbed Veema round the throat and dragged her backwards into the cabin, a shortwave stunner held to her head. Without even looking at Camille, Moss closed the door on them, and shouted down the corridor, "Now, Elnac!"

This had better work, or we'll have a hostage situation on our hands, he thought. He hoped Veema wouldn't panic before Elnac reacted.

"Was it a success, Elnac?" Moss called

"There's enough nicene gas in the cabin now to fell a rhino."

"I hope you didn't use too much."

"How the hell should I know. I've never used it before."

"Get Bartok to bring two respirators and two restraining bonds down to me."

Bartok came running ponderously down the corridor. "Here you are, boss."

"Right, respirators on, and be ready to follow me in." Moss pulled on his respirator and opened the door.

Even through the filters he could smell the dry pungency of the nicene. The pumps were working hard to dispel it.

Camille lay sprawled lengthways on the floor, with Veema alongside her. The stunner had ended up on the far corner of the bunk. Moss saw it and picked it up. He couldn't let Camille get her hands on it again. Veema had obviously cracked her head against the washbasin when she fell; the impact had knocked her unconscious. A livid bruise was forming over her right eye. Camille groaned.

"Get those straps on her, Bartok, while I move Veema."

Moss dragged Veema out of the cabin, while Bartok immobilized Camille by strapping up her wrists and ankles.

Veema seemed so frail. Moss propped her up against the corridor wall, afraid that he might have overdone the gas. He slapped her face, his heart pounding. No response. He was about to do it again, when her eyelids fluttered.

"You bastard!" she said thickly, and then was wracked by a fit of coughing.

★ ★ ★

Preston stared into the aquarium in the corner of his office. One of the engineers, working on the sea intake valves that provided water for the generators, had found some strange creatures in the pipe-work. Individually, they were only about twenty millimetres long, and they seemed to glow silver. The disquieting thing about them was that, occasionally, they would bunch together into a ball. They each had two lidless eyes. These stared out from under rainbow-coloured, translucent filaments that protruded, like shrimps' legs, from one end of their ovoid bodies. They were bunching together now, as if they sensed that something was about to happen. With those little staring eyes looking at him, Preston felt a cold shiver down his back. He heard the office door slide open but he purposely didn't look round immediately. He knew who it would be. He composed himself.

"Well?" Berbek's voice.

"Well, what?"

"Years of research and millions of pounds of government funding, Preston, and how far have you got?"

"We've traced Loratu back into the past."

"But you still don't know how he got there, do you?" said Berbek. "And, you still don't know what made him start the revolution."

"Now, there, I think you're wrong," said Preston.

"I was pretty sure you'd been keeping something from me."

"Look, General, there's nothing sinister in this. We need to test transference back into the past. It's not easy. In fact, it's damned difficult."

"Difficult or not, Preston, you've had enough time to test everything, and do it more than once. I'm taking over. This installation will now be run on military lines, and the direction of the research will be guided by me."

"Impossible!" Preston was horrified at the idea of someone like Berbek taking over his work.

"Face it, Preston, you've not been getting results. I want Loratu to cease to exist."

"And, how do you propose to motivate my team, if I don't choose to help you, which I don't?"

"A gun at the side of the head works wonders," said Berbek firmly. "Already, my men are moving into position around the central core of your installation, like it or not."

"And where do I fit into all this?"

"You will work directly at my command."

"And, if I don't?"

"You used to be a redhead, didn't you? It's a very specific gene that gives rise to red hair. Berbek put a hand into the top, left-hand pocket of his flak jacket and pulled out a small silver phial. "One injection of the contents of this, and you will begin to die horribly, as your D.N.A starts to regress."

A tinny murmur came over Berbek's head-set. He spoke briefly into the microphone and then said to Preston, "It seems my men have discovered a metal door, deep underground. Should they cut it open, do you think?"

"So, you do need my help, after all," Preston sneered.

"No, but it would be simpler all round to have it. Shall we go?"

"There is very fragile equipment behind that door. I don't want your heavies trampling all over it."

"And, it's top-secret as well, I suppose?"

"You certainly wouldn't want everyone to know about it," said Preston.

"Hmm." Berbek stood looking at the floor for a moment, then his head came up. "So, Camille didn't make it, then."

"What?"

"Loratu's onto her. Is anyone closer to you than that woman is? You're such a cold fish, aren't you, Preston? But nobody does it for you like she does. So, now we have a common goal: we both want Loratu simply to cease to exist."

"I will open that door for you, then."

"Good."

"But on one condition," said Preston.

"Now, I hardly think..."

"Kill me and you'll never get to Loratu, my friend," he said sarcastically.

"Ah, but that's the beauty of it. I don't kill you, just make you a little… what shall we say? Uncomfortable, by slow degrees."

"Your elite force is all linked together by surgical implants, yes?"

Berbek nodded.

"The electrical interference inside the core project will give each of them an extremely nasty headache. They'll have to stay outside, when we go in."

"Oh, very well. Let's get on with it, shall we?"

The lift was small and antiquated. Preston pulled the latticework lift doors shut, the lift shuddered and, with a loud whine of machinery, began to descend.

"It's down three levels, through the rock. The tunnelling skills of the Nazis were really quite remarkable," Preston shouted above the din.

Berbek merely nodded. He was beginning to feel claustrophobic.

"Loratu tried three times to go back in time. The first time he did so, I think was a mistake. He delivered the information on how to do it to himself, but it was when he was only a boy. Of course, being so young, he didn't understand what he had, but I imagine a vestige of the concept stayed with him. He got back in time as far as his grandfather, but that didn't do any good either. Finally, he got the information back to himself when he was aged twenty, and working on Eurocom One. That was where you'd given him a job, incidentally. The whole thing has a nice symmetry about it, don't you think?"

Symmetry, be damned, thought Berbek. This man's ego is becoming insufferable. The lift finally ground to a halt. Preston heaved the creaking lattice open. Berbek was heartily glad to be out of there, but the heat at this depth was unexpected.

They found themselves in a tunnel that was badly lit by a few naked light bulbs. Huge, insulated pipes snaked along the walls. Cables hung in loops from the ceiling. The atmosphere was oppressive, and filled with the reek of ozone.

"Down here," said Preston, leading the way, "is where we have the core of Project Alpha."

They rounded the corner. Armed guards stood along the sides of the corridor and flanked a heavy iron door set in the rock. Berbek strode over to the sergeant in charge.

"Take your men back up the corridor. I want them well clear of this door, when we open it."

"Sir. And then, sir?"

"Just keep clear until I call you."

"Sir!" The sergeant saluted smartly.

"Get this thing open, will you, Preston?" Berbek was sweating now. This had better be worth it, he thought.

"My pleasure." Preston leaned forward and turned a lever set in the centre of the door. He pulled back on it, the door creaked open, and let Berbek lead the way to the other side. Preston bowed mockingly at his broad back.

They emerged onto a walkway, high above the floor of a cave. Below them, avenues of equipment and workbenches radiated like the spokes of a wheel from a central platform. On this platform sat a rectangular framework, about six by three by six metres, painted in red oxide. There was an unfinished air about it.

"Is that all it is, then?" said Berbek, thinking he was being made a fool of.

"What did you expect?"

"Something a bit more exciting than this, for all the money we've been pumping in."

"You mean, you thought there would be flashing lights,

electric cables, and huge electrodes. Yes, yes, that sort of stuff looks good in the vids, but this is science in the raw."

Preston strode down the metal staircase, with Berbek, in his studded boots, clanking down behind him. There was no doubt whose kingdom this was. Preston led the way down the avenue of technicians, who were bending over oscilloscopes and computer terminals. Berbek thought some of the equipment looked rather ancient. Where had all the money gone?

"When it's ready," said Preston, raising his voice against the background hum, "these stanchions, by which I mean, the box-frame, will hold a temporal field. A volunteer will sit on a chair in the middle. We haven't yet figured out how to send anything animate yet, but we think we can transmit consciousness back in time, into a suitable host."

Berbek went up the concrete steps and into the box-frame. He looked around. What was Preston doing behind his back? Was he signalling to somebody? Berbek went to take a step forward, and found that he couldn't move. What the hell was going on? He spoke into his headset microphone. "Sergeant, bring your men in here immediately."

He saw Preston smile. "He won't hear you. There is a dampening field in operation."

"What are you going to do?" Berbek asked, beginning to panic.

"You are the man who wanted to see where all the money's gone. I'm giving you a firsthand experience."

A blue glow sprang up between the red metal posts of the box-frame. Berbek struggled to free his feet, and then realized that he only had to undo the straps, to get out of his boots, but it was already too late for that. The blue light changed to a coruscating orange. The air filled with static.

Berbek began to choke.

"Get... me... out... of... here!" he shouted, between fits of coughing. All he could see was Preston, who was bending down and looking at a computer screen. A technician was sitting beside him, typing in some instructions. Berbek looked down at his hands, and saw, in horror, that age spots were fast appearing. His eyesight was growing dim. All around him the vortex roared faster and faster. He put his hands up to his head, and clumps of white hair came away in his fingers. His hands were turning skeletal. With a final scream, his consciousness exploded.

– 12 –

Agent Emerald

The images were so powerful that Moss froze in the act of tending to Veema. Berbek was trapped in a tornado of orange and mauve luminescence, inside the bars of a tall, box-like structure. His huge frame sagged and bent. His hair turned white, his face became skull-like and sickly yellow. Berbek uttered a scream that penetrated the spinning vortex of light. His skeletal, and now blackening, corpse exploded. The whirlwind ceased, and Moss found himself looking down on some blackened fragments, out of which Berbek's charred skull leered up at him. The thought reverberated in Moss's head: this is pay back time, General.

Next came a warning. Well, it said, Mr. Moss, you're next. The image of the charred remains faded. Moss expected to find fluid exuding from his skull and leaking between his fingers, as he clutched his head, which was now aching almost beyond endurance. He found himself sitting down in the corridor, slumped against the wall, bending over Veema, who had her head against his chest. His eyes were streaming.

The susurration came again. "We are ssorry. The sstrength of the one man's fear and the other man'ss triumph overwhelmed uss momentarily. We were in your mind, watching him and the man Berbek, at the same time."

"Who was this other man?"

"The man whose mind you were in was Preston. He had just ended the life of General Berbek, having lured him into a rudimentary kind of time machine."

"And now, he intends to kill me? Why does he have to do that?"

"He sees you as a threat. He is going to send someone's mind back in time, to kill Veema's grandmother, so you and your Veema will never have existed."

"How is that possible?"

"We do not know yet. We must leave you now."

Moss rested his painful head against the cool, steel plating of the corridor wall. He felt Veema stir in his arms.

"You bastard!" she said again.

"Thank God, you're back," he said.

"Why the hell did you gas me?" she asked.

He stroked her forehead, in a gesture of apology. He struggled to speak through the pain. "I had to be sure about Camille. I knew there was a mole in the organization," he said faintly. "That much I have managed to remember." He swallowed, to try and clear his very dry throat.

She looked up at him. "You look awful."

"That makes... two of us."

"What happened about Camille? Was she the mole?"

"Very probably. I didn't want a hostage situation, and... Berbek's dead. I'll explain everything later. My head hurts too much now."

"You'd better explain later. You could have killed me, couldn't you?"

"I don't know what else I could have done. Anything could have happened if I'd left you with her," Moss said, speaking slowly and with extreme difficulty.

After a while, Veema said thoughtfully, "You're sure now? There might be more like her in our group."

"You're not one. I know that now."

"You're certain about that?"

He didn't reply but took her in his arms, hugged her to him and gently kissed her bruised forehead.

After a while, she said, "How do you know that Berbek's dead?"

"I saw it happen. God, my head hurts!"

There was a respectful cough, and Elnac asked, "Er, boss, what're we going to do now?"

"Give me a minute, Elnac. Go back to the controls." Moss had begun to think about what they should do next, when the voices returned.

"We know how Presston'sss going to eliminate you."

Moss leant for support on Veema. He dimly saw her looking into his face, concerned, but he couldn't hear her words.

"In one hour, Presston will begin the experiment. He has the knowledge to persuade Veema's grandmother that her husband is having an affair with Sally Price, which will motivate the woman to kill Sally."

"What can I do to stop him?"

"At the moment of transference, you will – how do you say this – piggy-back that person's mind into the past. Once you are there, we will no longer be able to help you."

"Will I be to able come back to the present?"

"We don't know."

The voices withdrew. Moss found he had collapsed on the floor. Someone was snapping their fingers in front of his face. He opened his eyes. Veema was bending over him. His voice came out cracked and dry. He said, "Veema, he's going to kill you in one hour from now. I have to try to prevent it."

"How can you do that?"

"They're sending me back into the past... my mind, I mean, into some else's mind."

Veema stared at him. "What if you don't come back?"

He held her gaze. "If I don't go, neither of us will exist, and perhaps others, too, will never be."

"Have they told you of any precautions you can take?"

"No. Wait a minute. There is something." He put his hand to his head. "Wearing the time jacket will provide some protection. It will create a field that will protect me in the present, and may prevent a time-loop being established. I wish I still had that jacket now."

A huge smile spread over Veema face. "Then, there is something I can do for you. You gave me the jacket – remember?"

"You've still got it? How's that possible?" Moss said, his hopes renewed.

"It's a long story. Remind me to tell it to you someday." She suddenly became very businesslike.

"Bartok," she shouted, "come and help me get the boss to his bunk."

Together, they carried him along the corridor and into his cabin.

"I'll be back in a moment," she said.

Elnac stood there, looking at Moss.

"If you're gonna be out cold, we need ter know what ter do next, and who's in charge here."

"Tell Elnac to take the ship to the Jubilee bunker, and you'll both be taking take your orders from Veema. I'm holding Elnac personally responsible for Camille. She could still be very dangerous."

"Right, boss. I'd – er – better get back to the cockpit."

Veema returned with the time jacket. "Get into this and lie down. Then, I'll plug you into the ship's power source."

As soon as he had put the jacket on, he felt its soothing warmth, then his head began to clear. The pain ebbed away, but something odd was happening to him. Veema must have seen this because she knelt on the floor and put her hands to either side of his head. She kissed him on the forehead.

"Goodbye, my love. Come back to me."

The image of her face faded into blackness, and he felt horribly alone. He tried to remember every last thing about her, just in case he never saw her again.

★ ★ ★

Eva's hands were busy with some knitting. She looked up and found herself in a comfortable sitting room suffused with warm sun. She looked at the clock. Moss, inside her mind, thought, this is not really me. *Eva Moss* is doing all these things. She's thinking, it's half past three. Where can he be, that husband of mine? George and Irene are coming at four. Then Eva shouted aloud, surprising Moss with her vehemence.

"I know where he is, the bastard! He's with that woman in the park. They've been at it for ages, months, maybe longer. She's with him now, the hussy! How dare they! I'll show her! Nobody pinches my husband and gets away with it."

Moss was aware of the extraordinarily white hot anger surging through her whole body. He kept on having to remind himself that it wasn't his body. It was very confusing. Every action of her body, he interpreted automatically as his. But, he also knew that she was under another influence, and it was his mission to counteract it.

Eva got up. Her skirt flapped against her legs, and it felt most peculiar to Moss, to be inside the mind and body of a woman. Eva went out of the room, across the sunlit hall and into the kitchen. She opened a drawer, took out a long, serrated knife and went back into the hall. She fitted the knife length-wise into a black, shiny bag with long straps. She looked at herself in the hall mirror, and Moss saw a woman in her late forties, with greying, severely curled hair and a pale, heavily pink-powdered face looking back at him. The mouth was turned down at the corners, and the eyes were determined. She took a lipstick from her bag and smeared her lips. She tied a square of material round her head, and opened the front door. She put on a pair of sunglasses, slammed the door behind her and strode off down the road. She stopped after a few paces.

"Oh! What a stupid girl I am! I've still got my slippers on," she said. She returned to the house and changed into brown, flat, lace-up shoes. Then she set out again. Moss could feel her determination boiling over. So far, he had not been able to have any effect on her at all. There was an impenetrable force between him and her consciousness, and he was aware of it reinforcing her anger.

She walked rapidly down the road, until she came to an intersection where there were white bars painted on the tarmac. Opposite each other, on either side of the road, there were poles painted alternately black and white, with orange globes on top. On the far side of the road there was parkland. A large hut stood next to a high wooden gate. Vehicles, probably of the petrol-engine type Moss had read about, passed by at dizzying speed, belching smoke and fumes. How would one get across through this traffic, Moss wondered? Obviously, Eva knew how to do it. She coughed, for no apparent reason.

A strange sensation ran through her body. Why did I cough, she wondered. I didn't want to cough. Moss knew the reason. He had always found strong fumes made him cough. He realised that he possibly had some sort of control over Eva's physical actions, and he hoped he might be able to make use of this.

Eva shrugged her shoulders. What did it matter, anyway? She looked left and right, and then stepped out onto the road. For a moment, Moss panicked. She'll get herself killed! But the vehicles stopped for her. He felt a surge of relief.

She walked quickly across the road and up to the gate-keeper's hut. She produced a ticket from her bag and handed it to the gate-keeper through a hole in the glass.

"Lovely day, isn't it?" the man said, handing it back.

When she spoke, Moss was surprised to discover that her voice was high pitched, but not unpleasant.

"I wish it was," she said.

"Something the matter?"

She didn't reply.

"Well, mind how you go."

She passed through the turnstile, marched up a path and into the trees. Moss was so taken by the myriad sights, smells and feelings that were crowding in on him, that it took a while for the full implication of his marvellous discovery to dawn on him. If he could make Eva cough to order, what else might he make her do?

Eva muttered to herself, as she stomped angrily across the park. "They'll be in that coppice, lying together on her rug, canoodling, the dirty beasts."

He felt her take a firmer grip on her bag and go striding through the trees, her whole body shaking with rage. The sound of her blood pumping in her ears made Moss deaf. A red mist had come down over her eyes. Panicking, Moss thought, I must do something now, before it's too late. She's going to kill Veema's grandmother. Oh, Veema, darling Veema, I won't let you down.

Eva was inhaling deeply through her nose and exhaling through her mouth, dragging in the oxygen she would need to do the deed. She stopped, cocked her head to one side and listened carefully. Her breathing slowed. Creeping forward, watching her footing, she parted the foliage in front of her. She could hear little giggles and murmurs of pleasure to her right. The sun back-lit a canopy of branches. They hung almost to the ground and were all that separated her from her husband and his lover.

Eva removed her sunglasses and dropped them on the ground. She took the knife from her bag and held it point downwards. Very gently, she parted the leaves a little.

Now, little Eva, you know exactly where to aim for; between the ribs and into the heart.

Moss realised, in desperation, that the other consciousness was making itself more strongly felt. It mustn't know that he was there, too. He had to do something... anything, to distract her.

She moved forward remorselessly. There was the other woman, her back turned towards her. She was wearing a long dress, and Eva's husband was in the act of unbuttoning it.

One clean stroke, little Eva, and she will die slowly and painfully, as her lifeblood drains away, oozing over his hands.

Eva moved forwards through the curtain of leaves, poised to strike. Moss put all his mental energy into making her cough. He would do *anything* to distract her. But she was moving too fast; the blade was flashing in the sunshine.

She was overwhelmed by a series of wracking coughs.

Sally looked towards Eva, and Moss saw her mouth open in a soundless scream. It was Veema's face.

Eva's husband threw himself at Eva, and knocked her to the ground. She fell heavily and lost consciousness.

Dimly, Moss heard birdsong and the sighing of the wind.

★ ★ ★

Eva came slowly back to consciousness and saw a man looking down at her. Moss had been able to distance himself from her mind while she was knocked out. The other controlling mind, that had been holding him back, seemed to have let go of her. Moss found his voice and croaked, "Veema, are you all right?" The woman screamed and went on screaming.

★ ★ ★

In the shuttle-craft, Veema screamed, "He's going!"

She watched helplessly as Moss's body thrashed about in a fit. Then, suddenly, he stopped. His eyes began to move ceaselessly behind his closed eyelids. Bracing herself, she slapped his face. And again.

"I can't wake him up!"

Bartok went down on his knees and placed his ear to Moss's chest. "He's breathin' OK."

"Why won't you wake up?"

"We have to get him to a doctor," Bartok said.

"But where can we take him?"

"We're on our way to the Jubilee bunker, aren't we?

Dalziel's going to be there."

"Get onto him, then, and tell him what's happened to the Boss."

"Right you are." He ran off down the corridor. Moss's body twitched.

★ ★ ★

In Preston's medical complex, the man on the operating table twitched.

"What's happening?" Preston turned to Ackroyd his chief medical officer.

"I don't know." Ackroyd looked at the brain wave patterns on the screen and he felt the man's pulse. A forest of multicoloured wires were attached to pads all over the man's shaved head. The man's hands convulsed feebly. His eyes moved about furiously behind the closed lids.

"I've never seen these brainwave patterns before, but we're going way beyond the frontiers of what we know. We could lose this one."

"Then we'll get another one," said Preston, looking up at him.

★ ★ ★

Bob Moss and Sally Price looked down in fear at Moss's wife Eva. Her body twitched, but the hand round the knife remained clenched.

Bob said quietly, "How could she have known about us?"

"She knows. That's all that matters, darling. Shouldn't you telephone for an ambulance, or something?"

"Yes, right. Are you sure you'll be OK if I leave you here?" he said.

"I'll be all right, but please hurry. I'd better go, hadn't I? I shouldn't be here when the ambulance men arrive."

"Right. I'll – er – give you a call."

★ ★ ★

Bob ran, struggling through undergrowth, falling over several times, until he reached the gate. He emerged, muddy and dishevelled. The man inside the hut looked at him with distaste.

"There's…" He paused to recover his breath, "There's been an accident; get an ambulance."

"Calm down, sir. What's this all about?"

"It's my wife," he blurted out.

The man gave him a strange look, but said nothing. He ponderously dialled 999.

The minutes dragged by. Then Bob heard a furiously ringing bell, and the long white ambulance lurched up to the gates. Bob had been so agitated that he'd forgotten they were closed. He rushed over and dragged them open. The ambulance drove through and halted.

"Where's your wife, sir?"

"In the wood over there."

"Lead the way, sir."

All the way to the hospital, he kept asking, "She's going to be all right, isn't she?"

The ambulance man, riding in the back with him, would only say, "We'll soon be there, sir."

Bob held Eva's clammy hand. She seemed to be in the throes of a bad dream from which she could not wake.

* * ★

"How long before we get there?" Veema looked up anxiously as Bartok came in. Elnac was still at the controls.

"We're going as fast as we can."

"But how long will it take?"

"Elnac says about another twenty minutes."

"He has called the base hasn't he? He has spoken to Dalziel?"

"No. He doesn't want to break radio silence."

"You watch the boss. I've got to speak to Elnac."

She ran along the corridor into the cockpit.

"Get Dalziel on a secure a channel."

"Keep your 'air on. I already spoke to 'im. He's on line now."

Dalziel's voice, slightly distorted by static, came over the speaker, "Is that you, Veema?"

"Yes, it's me."

"Is he still having fits?"

"No, he's calm, but he won't wake up."

"In that case, stop trying to wake him. Otherwise, you say, he appears stable?"

"Yes, except that his eyes keep moving."

"Try not to worry. I've got everything ready. The moment you land, I'll be at the docking bay with a stretcher."

Veema went back to sit with Moss. She held his hand for what seemed an eternity, stroking it, willing him awake. At the edge of her thoughts, she heard the steady rhythm of engines change to a high-pitched whine, and then there was a sensation of falling. The craft settled clumsily and the engines shut off. The next she knew, Dalziel was peering over her shoulder. She looked up at him pleadingly. Dalziel leant over Moss, pulled back an eyelid, and shone a light into the pupil. Then he tried the other eye.

Veema grabbed him by the forearm. "What do you think?"

"Let's get him out of here and into the Medlab. We need to take a proper look at him. You take his feet and I'll take him under the arms. Lift now!"

Together, they got him out of the craft, down the ramp and onto the waiting trolley.

"What happened?" Dalziel asked.

Veema didn't know whether she should tell even a part of the story. The more she thought about it, the more fantastic it seemed. She concentrated on helping Dalziel to push the trolley. She decided that she had to tell him part of the story.

"The thing is, Dalziel, that Preston is conducting experiments into time. He's able, we think, to send someone's consciousness back in time, but we've no proof. Loratu said he was going back in time, to try to prevent a murder; and now he won't wake up."

"Sounds incredible, but I've known still stranger things happen in medicine," Dalziel said thoughtfully.

They pushed the trolley through scratched, plastic, double doors and into the medical facility.

"The first thing we need to do is to get him hooked up to some diagnostic equipment," Dalziel said, and pulled back the sheet that had been covering Moss up to the chin. "What's this thing he's wearing?"

"It's a time jacket," said Veema.

"I've heard of these things, but I've never seen one before. Why's he in it? What does it do?"

"It's something to do with saving him. I can't really explain. All I know is, we mustn't remove it."

"All right."

Working quickly and methodically, Dalziel wired Moss's scalp up to an array of monitors. He attached a bulldog clip device over Moss's right index finger, to test the amount of oxygen in his bloodstream. Electrical pulses traced their intricate paths across various screens.

"That's interesting," Dalziel said, thoughtfully.

"What?" Veema asked anxiously.

"Some years ago, I did some work on the theory of the collective unconscious. I put an implant in the hypothalamus of six volunteers, and then fed an electrical impulse into one of them. Oddly, all of them reacted to this in the same way; if one rolled over, they all rolled over."

"That's more than odd. How did you get them out of their trance?"

"I couldn't."

"Oh." Veema sat down heavily on a metal stool. She began to cry, slowly at first, then losing all control.

"He means a lot to you, doesn't he?"

Veema raised a tear-stained face to him and nodded silently. She sniffed, and wiped her eyes with the back of her hand.

"The only thing I know," he said slowly, "and I don't know exactly, but, the theory is that…"

"Go on," she said, when he hesitated.

"The collective unconscious is in balance. In order to take someone out, you have to put someone else in."

Veema sat very quietly, trying to understand what he was telling her. Then, her head came up and she looked at him squarely.

"In other words, for him ever to wake up, you have to link him to another person's consciousness?"

Dalziel nodded.

"Can you recreate your experiment?"

"I expect I can, yes. It would be much more difficult to do, without my notes, but I can try."

"Good. I know what to do now."

"What?" Dalziel asked, surprised.

"Can you extract some nanites from Loratu's bloodstream?"

"*Nanites?* What's going on?"

"You'll see."

★ ★ ★

Preston's chief medical officer, Ackroyd, came over to Preston, who was sitting beside the unconscious body of the man on the operating table.

Preston looked up gloomily. "Yes?"

"You'll have noticed Engelmann's brainwave patterns."

"Of course. What of them?"

"Don't you recognize them?"

Preston looked closely at the screen, "I see nothing but very ordinary alpha waves."

Ackroyd keyed in a sequence of commands on the keypad beside the screen. "Now what do you see?"

"What have you done?" asked Preston.

"Brought together all the output signals from all the points wired on his body."

"How and when did you see the significance of these output signals?"

"I had an idea about it some time ago. What do you make

of the multiple patterns, Preston?"

"Shared activities of some kind," said Preston. He thought for a moment. "You don't mean Engelmann, Loratu and Eva Moss are all linked in some way?"

"Yes. That's how it looks."

"So, you mean to say that what is known to one will be known to the other two?"

"Yes. Don't you agree that it's possible?"

Preston sat with his hand over his mouth for some time. "This needs a lot of thought. We can't wake up Engelmann just like that."

"I don't think we will ever be able to wake him up."

"So what do we do about Loratu? We have to do something."

"We have to bring him here. We have no choice."

"Impossible!" said Preston. "How are we even going to find him?"

"I don't know. But we really need to know what's going on with him, if we're ever going to make progress with Eva Moss."

"Obviously Engelmann wasn't successful."

"Why do you say that?"

"He was programmed to wake up as soon as he had completed his mission."

A technician came running into the room and said, "Sir, Agent Emerald, on an open line."

"What? Punch it through here."

"Yes, sir."

The technician ran off. Ackroyd and Preston exchanged amazed glances. The screen in front of them flickered into life. The picture quality was poor and wavered, but it was recognisably Camille Blanche.

Preston leant close to the screen. "Where are you?"

"Loratu's Jubilee base."

"Are you OK?"

"She's fine." Veema's face appeared alongside. "This is a scrambled line, before you get any ideas about trying to track us."

Without looking away from the screen, Preston wrote on a pad in front of him, 'Get a fix on this.'

"Now, what makes you think I want to track you?"

"Whatever! I wouldn't bother trying, if I were you." Preston looked over to Ackroyd, who shook his head.

"Listen, Preston, we have a proposition for you. Share your information about how you send consciousness back into the past with us, and we might all find a way out of this mess."

"What is it you want me to do, exactly?"

"Is your equipment transportable?"

"If you have sufficient power, yes."

"Moss says that you have someone there and have already sent his mind into the past. Bring that man to us."

"No deal."

"Is Agent Emerald expendable, or can we use her for our purposes, if we can't have your man?"

Veema moved slightly, so that Preston could see the gun pressed to the side of Camille's head.

"Are you proposing a trade?" Preston asked.

"Yes. Your patient and your equipment in exchange for Emerald."

"If I agree, what do you think you can do with them?"

"Loratu, Eva Moss and your man are all locked in stasis. You sent someone back in time, to kill my grandmother. I'm still here aren't I? Something must have gone wrong with your plan. Together, we can resolve this situation."

"How?"

"Bring everything here and we'll show you how."

"What will you do if I don't?"

"Then, we're all stuck, and your precious Camille dies."

Camille suddenly came to life. "She won't let me die."

"Oh, I will. I love Loratu far more than Preston could ever love you."

The picture widened to include Dalziel, who added, "And if you have any doubts about Veema doing it, I certainly will."

Preston grimaced at Dalziel's image. "You were supposed to be dead."

"And it's no thanks to you that I'm not."

"But Camille saved your life."

"Well, now I'll save hers, if you'll co-operate. Otherwise....."

"D'you expect an answer now?"

"Leave it longer than an hour, and, make no mistake about this, she dies."

The picture flickered off.

Ackroyd pushed a hand through his sandy hair and looked at Preston. "You're not going to do it?"

"I don't have much choice."

"Camille's that important to you?"

"Not really, but this gives me a chance to get close to Loratu and Veema. I've got to take it."

Ackroyd looked at him hard. "Well, we'd better get the equipment ready."

★ ★ ★

Moss stared about him. White mist swirled everywhere. Then he heard someone clear their throat. He saw a tall, bald man with piercing grey eyes, who was looking at him closely.

"So, you're Loratu."

"And you are?"

"Julius Engelmann, Preston's guinea pig. Looks like we're in this mess together."

"Where's that Eva woman?"

"Eva Moss? Somewhere around, but too frightened to show herself. At least we know what's going on; she doesn't."

"How do we get out of here?" asked Moss.

"I don't know."

Far off, they heard a woman crying. Then the mist parted and Eva was there.

"I'm dreaming; you aren't I?" Eva said unhappily.

"No, I'm afraid you're not dreaming," said Engelmann.

"This is difficult to explain," Moss said, "but he and I are from the future."

"Where am I?"

"We don't know," said Moss.

"We think we're all in your head," said Engelmann.

Suddenly, Moss had an idea. It seemed to come unbidden.

"If we ever get out of here, I want you to divorce your husband and move away from your area."

"I've every intention of getting rid of that slimy toad," she said, vehemently.

"But the moving away is important. You must forget all about Sally Price, and you must never set eyes on her again."

"But…"

"Repeat after me: 'I will never see Sally Price again. I will forget all about her. She never existed. My husband committed adultery with a woman he prefers not to name. I must tell him that. I must tell him to confess to that, in writing, and then I must go away – right away.' Understand?"

"I will forget about that woman, get him to sign an agreement and I will go away," she said tonelessly. Then she faded out of sight.

"Very clever," said Engelmann. "It might just work. I shall have to tell Preston about this, you know."

"Yes, I'm sure you will, but hypnotic suggestion can be very strong, remember. You may not be able to break it."

"I'm not going inside her mind again, not for anything!" said Engelmann, "that's if I ever get out of here."

★ ★ ★

Elnac bent over the controls in the bunker's ops room.

"How's it going?" Bartok said.

"See that blip there, that's Preston's shuttle."

"So he gave in after all?"

"I don't think so. He's just hoping to make a bad situation better by getting close to the boss, so he can do something to him."

Bartok grinned. "So I'd better keep close to his throat."

"You and me both."

"But won't he give our position away to the authorities? They would still love to get their hands on us."

"That's a risk Veema's is prepared to take. With Berbek out of the way, no one's come forward yet to take 'is place. Preston just does one thing at a time. Right now, he's after the boss and Veema, if you ask me."

"What about Miss Smarty Pants?" said Bartok.

"Let's have a look at her, shall we?" Elnac switched the view to show Camille as she lay on her bunk, still restrained at her wrists and ankles.

Bartok grunted. "Don't look too pleased, do she?"

The perimeter alarm klaxon sounded.

"It looks like our visitors are about to arrive," said Elnac. "Time to put her to sleep."

"Shouldn't we ask Veema about this, first?"

"Nar. Why should she have all the fun?"

Moments later, Camille lay unconscious, her cabin flooded with Nicene gas.

"Nighty night!" said Bartok.

★ ★ ★

Moss could smell disinfectant and hear many voices, some near, some far off, echoing. Whistling. Doors banging. He couldn't open his eyes. Where am I and where's Engelmann? he wondered,

"I think that I must be in hospital,"

"Yes, we're in the Infirmary," Moss said, recognising Eva's voice.

"Oh, you're still with me, then?"

"I suppose I must be; you can hear my thoughts?" Moss said, surprised.

"Yes."

"I'd better be careful, then. Do you know where Engelmann is?"

"That other man?"

"Yes."

"Oh, I didn't like him. I don't want to listen to him."

"You mean, you can choose who you listen to?"

"I suppose so. Anyway, you're not real are you? I'm not unconscious anymore. I'm in full control, aren't I?"

"Come on Mrs. Moss. Wake up. It's all right. You're safe now."

The eyes that were not Moss's eyes suddenly opened. A man in a white coat was leaning over her. He had some sort of instrument round his neck and dangling down his chest.

Could that be a stethoscope? How archaic! Moss thought.

"How archaic," Eva said, without thinking.

"What was that?" the doctor's smile vanished.

"Nothing. It was just something that man said."

"What man?"

"The man in my head."

The doctor shouted, "Nurse!"

"Yes, doctor," said a nurse, hurrying over to him.

He moved away and spoke to her in whispers. Then he came back.

"Nurse'll just get you a nice cup of tea. I'll be back in a moment."

The nurse smiled encouragingly. Moss studied her. White starched hat on black curls, pretty round face, brown eyes, small nose. Her pale blue dress, buttoned down the front, had a white apron pinned to it. Encircling her waist was a black belt. Her short sleeves ended in white cuffs. Fascinating and very sexy. He would introduce that uniform and make all the pretty girls wear it, if he ever got back, he told himself.

"Here's your tea, dear."

"I'm not your dear," said Eva, truculently.

"I'm sorry, just a figure of speech."

"Yes, well. Any biscuits?"

"No, sorry." The nurse turned on her heel and left.

"Hah, that saw her off! What did you think of *that*, Mister whatever your name is?"

"Moss."

"Hmm. Moss. Doesn't sound very futuristic to me. This tea tastes revolting. Still, what can you expect on the N.H.S these days?"

"N.H.S?"

Eva gulped down some more tea. "National Health Service. You ought to know that if as you're a…"

"Figment."

"Yes, a figment of my imagination. Well, the best that can be said for *that* was it was wet and warm. I do feel sleepy, all of a sudden." She yawned widely, put her cup down on the side cupboard and snuggled under the covers. "I'll just take forty winks." And she was gone. The mist was back.

★ ★ ★

"Bit unethical of them, wasn't it?" Engelmann said, smiling sardonically.

"Well, they must have thought she was raving. And we're still no further forward."

"Preston'll get me out now she's unconscious."

"Perhaps, he'll get us both out."

"I doubt that. Only one of us will be able to leave; anyway, he wants you dead."

★ ★ ★

"They're here!" said Elnac, over the intercom.

Veema looked up wearily and rubbed her eyes. Moss lay immobile in the medlab, hooked up to an array of equipment, only his eyes were moving ceaselessly under their lids.

"OK. I'm coming." She turned to Dalziel, who was sitting

beside her, and asked, "Have you got those nanites ready for injection into Preston?"

"Yes. Now, remember, that patch on your finger contains a very fast-acting anaesthetic. Be very careful to press it firmly onto his bare skin. It's effect is not long-lasting, so we'll have to get Preston back here quickly."

"I understand." She bent down and kissed Moss on the forehead. "I won't be long, my love." She got up, stretched and left the room. Her calf muscles ached badly. To ease them, she walked quickly down the corridor that led down to the underground cave, where Preston's craft had docked. She approached to within a few metres of it and stopped, easing her muscles. With a hiss, the craft's port opened; from underneath it, a ramp extended onto the rock floor. Preston looked out.

"Where's Camille?"

Veema met his gaze stonily. "Locked up."

"I want to see her."

"Bring out the equipment and the patient, first."

"Not until I see her."

Veema spoke into her wristcom. "Bartok, Elnac, bring Agent Emerald down to the docking bay."

Elnac's voice sounded tinny over the small speaker. "We're on our way."

"And how is Mister Moss?" Preston sneered, a slight smile on his lips.

"*Loratu* is still in deep REM sleep, no thanks to you."

"So," Preston asked, "how do we break the stasis?"

"You'll have to ask Dalziel that," she said.

"Where is he?"

"Looking after Loratu. How do I know you've got your patient with you?"

Preston smiled. "Surely, your scans will have told you?"

"They tell us you've got another human being with you, but that's all. I want to see him."

"You can see him, when I see Camille."

There were footsteps behind Veema. She turned and saw Elnac and Bartok. They were wheeling a hospital trolley down the slope towards her. Camille was stretched out on it. Veema was angry that this pair had gassed Camille without her express permission, but nothing could be done about it now. It might even work to her advantage.

"What have you done to her?" shouted Preston, coming down the ramp. Veema moved forward quickly. This is probably the only chance I'll get, she thought, while he's off guard. She reached out, grasped his wrist just below his shirt cuff, and pressed the patch on her finger firmly onto his skin.

"Come and take a good look at our Sleeping Beauty. It's only the effect of the nicene gas. Satisfied?" Veema said, releasing him, without his even noticing what she had done to him.

"I'm going to do nothing until she's released into my care," he said, backing away from the trolley towards his shuttlecraft.

"Then, it seems we have a standoff. Elnac, Bartok, take her back to her cell."

She turned deliberately and walked back with them, ready for Preston's next move. She heard footsteps behind her as Preston broke into a run. He was almost on her, and she turned, ready to defend herself, but he collapsed before he got to her. She spoke into her wristcom, "Okay Dalziel, it's all going as planned so far. He's unconscious."

"I'm bringing a trolley for him, right away," he said.

"Elnac, take Camille back to her room. Bartok, you wait for Dalziel to come with the trolley for Preston, and then take him to the medlab. Make sure he's strapped up well."

Bartok grinned. "It'll be a pleasure."

Dalziel appeared with the trolley and they heaved Preston onto it. Bartok wheeled it away.

Veema grinned at Dalziel. "We'd better see what Preston's got in store for us in his ship."

They went first into the cockpit cabin. Beyond this was small room; in it was a man on a trolley. He appeared to be asleep. Every so often, he twitched, as if he were suffering from a nightmare. It brought it home to Veema how her lover must be suffering. It won't be long now, she thought.

The man's bald head was covered in multicoloured wires, all leading into a cable that entered a black box strapped around his waist. A drip stood by his head, and a needle attached to a tube had been inserted into his wrist. By the wall, on a bed, there was a strange collection of metal hoops, eighty millimetres apart, arranged widthways, forming the shape of the human body. The head end was roughly contoured into a face, with breathing holes for the mouth and nose. The whole thing looked as if it were made of brushed aluminium. It had a sinister look, like one of those medieval torture machines that she'd seen when she was doing historical research, which was one of her passions, before the rise of General Berbek.

Dalziel came over and said, "I don't know what to make of this strange thing, do you?"

"Maybe, this is what Preston uses for his time transference experiments."

"Could be, I suppose. It looks a bit frightening."

"My thoughts exactly."

"What's it doing here?"

"Perhaps he wouldn't trust anyone with it while he was gone," he suggested.

"More likely, he had plans of his own. Perhaps, he was planning to spirit me away as well as rescue Camille."

Dalziel rubbed his mouth with the back of his hand. It was a sign that his mind was working overtime "I hope we've put paid to that, anyway. We'd better get it and the patient back to the lab. Can you call up the muscle?"

When they got back, Preston was fully awake. His wrists and ankles had been bound with plastic strips. He looked up at Veema

"What are you going to do to me?"

"Don't tempt me," she said. "I'm just going to give you a small injection."

Preston looked terrified. "What for?"

"It'll do you no good to struggle."

Preston tried to squirm out of the way, but to no avail.

"There, all done." She put the hypo-spray down carefully in the metal dish. She could see that he was on the verge of screaming. Well, let him.

"Wha-what's-happening? I can hear voices in my head," he moaned.

"They're the Asgathi. They won't harm you – much. What do you know about the collective unconscious?"

Preston said nothing, but struggled in his bonds. Sweat was trickling down his face. "Whatever you call them, they're hurting me."

"If they are, you've brought it on yourself."

"How?"

"You're the one that started it all. You and Berbek wanted Loratu to be able to speak but not to say anything that made any sense. What a publicity coup for you that would be, you thought. I recognise the voice that sang to me when I was in my cell. It was your voice. Camille must have played the recording to me while I was asleep. It awoke the post hypnotic suggestion to plant the nanites on Loratu. And now, my friend, they're in you." She smiled. "Rather neat, don't you think?"

"But, how can I hear these voices?"

"The nanites had the wonderful side effect of scrambling Loratu's brain patterns, so that he could communicate with them. Now, you can hear them, too."

"What are you going to do?"

"Send you back to join Engelmann in 1950."

"Impossible. You don't know how to operate the equipment."

"No, but you do; and everything you know the Asgathi know. It'll be like following a trail of breadcrumbs for them."

"I won't tell you anything."

"Oh, yes you will, Preston." Veema picked up another hypo-spray. "Sodium Pentothal. I've got the recording equipment running. Let's see what you have to say."

★ ★ ★

Moss was dreaming. Engelmann's voice drifted to him through the swirling mist. "You're never going to get out of here."

That was Moss's awful fear; to be marooned here until his body died of sickness or old age. He had hoped to be rescued. He now saw that this was impossible.

"Nonsense," he said to Engelmann. "We're going to be all right."

"Only one of us can leave," Engelmann said, "and that person's going to be me."

"What makes you so sure?"

"Preston is going to put another man into the time dilator. That man will come and get me, and, afterwards, he will be stuck in here with you. What do I care about him, as long as I get out. He'll be a new companion for you. Won't that be nice?"

"Perhaps, we can both get out. We're both in Eva's mind. If someone brings that mind back to the future, we'll both be saved."

Engelmann's laugh seemed to echo all around him. "I don't think it works like that, Mr. Moss."

★ ★ ★

Veema sat beside Moss, one of his hands clasped in both of hers.

"It won't be long now, my love, I promise. Dalziel's going to link me up to your time. Wish me luck." She placed his hand gently back on the bed.

"This is madness," whispered Preston. "You'll kill us both."

She looked at him grimly. "I'm willing to take that chance."

She took off the jacket of her black trouser suit. The wires attached to her scalp pulled slightly as the thick cable attached to the control box linking her to Preston and Preston to Loratu stretched. She lay down on the operating table. Dalziel dabbed her upper arm, and inserted a needle and tube for the anaesthetic, so that she and Preston could be put to sleep at the same time. Dalziel lowered the Preston's metal-hooped structure over her. She was unable to stem the fear that washed over her as he put the mask over her face. It was like being entombed.

"Are you all right?" Dalziel asked.

Her voice inside the mask sounded very loud to her. "I've got to be, haven't I?"

"I'm switching on the current now. I'm giving you five minutes; after that, I'll bring you back to us, what ever happens. Good luck."

The structure began to hum. Energy swept over her in waves of prickling heat; at first, they were no worse than pins and needles, then, they gradually worsened until she cried out in pain. She dimly heard Preston cry out too. White light. Blindness.

"I'm coming, my love. Wait for me." Her thoughts fled away.

★ ★ ★

Through the swirling mist, Veema, wearing a short, red skirt and a white blouse, half unbuttoned, walked towards Moss.

"Hello," he said.

"Hello, my love," she replied.

"I wish this wasn't a dream."

"It isn't."

"What?"

"I'm really here."

He looked her. "How can I tell?"

"Look into my mind. Some things have happened that you couldn't know have happened, and there are some things that only you and I would know about."

"How can I look into your mind?"

"I'm in here with you. Look, I'll show you."

He saw everything; how she had lured Preston into a trap.

"Now, we have to get you out."

"Moss is not going anywhere," said Engelmann, appearing through the mist.

"*Nobody's* going anywhere," said Preston, whose mind was now linked to theirs.

"Are you wearing a wristwatch?" Veema asked.

Preston checked. He was.

"Watch the minute hand. If I'm not back in three minutes, you'll be dead."

"That means I can come back," said Engelmann exultantly. "Only one of us has to stay behind."

Veema looked at him. "Exactly."

Preston threw himself at Engelman, and they fell, biting and kicking, out of sight.

Veema grabbed Moss's arm and pulled him towards her. "Look into my eyes," she said. "Whatever happens, don't close them and don't look away, however unpleasant it gets."

Veema's eyes filled his vision. He could feel her lips close on his, then her teeth biting. He cried out with the pain. He fell. Blinding, white light seared his brain. He could feel nothing, except the pain.

The back of his head felt as if it had been plunged into boiling water. He was suffocating. He couldn't open his eyes. Blackness. Aching blackness. He could feel himself thrashing about. He was breathing faster and faster. This is it, he thought, after all my travels, I'm finally going to die.

"Mr. Moss. Can you hear me?"

He opened his eyes. He could see. More than that, he

could *remember*.

"Dalziel, is that you?"

Dalziel smiled broadly. "So, you do remember me, after all. I *thought* it was just a trick."

"Where's Veema?" Moss said weakly.

"Over there."

Moss saw Veema lying on an operating table, an oxygen mask over her face. She looked very pale. Sweat glistened on her skin.

"Is she alright?"

"She will be. She's had a rough trip, In fact, you've both had a rough trip."

"What about Preston?"

"Dead."

"And Engelmann?"

"The same."

"Boss!" Elnac and Bartok came rushing triumphantly into the room. "Hey, are we going to have a party!"

"I know you. Bartok, isn't it? And you'll be Elnac?"

"Sure we are," said Elnac.

"What day is this?" Moss asked suddenly.

"Tuesday, September the third," said Dalziel.

"My birthday. What year is it?"

"Two thousand and fifty-three."

"Thank Gaia! I'm back."

– 13 –

Roentgen

"Deliver on your promisss." The Asgathi were back; Moss shuddered awake. The light level in the room was low and nobody was about. Veema lay asleep on a bed near him. A drip was in her arm.

Several days had passed since Moss's birthday, the day he regained his memory. They were still both feeling weak, but otherwise she said she was feeling a lot better. The pain in his head had faded. Without the time jacket, it would have taken much longer for him to feel better. Its gentle humming was comforting. His remaining problem was, that he felt giddy whenever he tried to stand. He looked at the clock by his bedside. Three am. Moss always felt at a low ebb, when he was awake at this hour of the night.

He focussed his thoughts on the Asgathi and asked, "What do you want me to do?"

"They are planning to send a space probe to Europa. You have to stop it. It will kill our *igmathu*… host family… home origin, core group… we don't have your words to describe what we mean. This probe will bring infectionss from your planet. We have no immunity It will destroy us."

"How do you suggest that I do this?"

"Now you are able to travel in time, you can go back and

reverse history."

"I don't think so. History has its own inertia. Suppose I were to succeed; you may withdraw from me. I still need your knowledge, to help me slow up the discovery of DNA. My world should not learn of it until it is more mature."

"We have restored your memory. That was our part of the bargain we made. You must now deliver on your promise."

"And if I don't?"

"Then, we can take your memory away again."

"I have to rely on you to help me if I manage to stop the probe. Once you've you've got what you want, I don't think you will be interested in helping me with DNA. What is mankind to you, after all?"

There was a silence, before the Asgathi spoke again. They told Moss, "We can live side by side with one another, but only if you can slow down space exploration."

"So, we need each other."

"Correct."

"I want the chance to try and improve my world, before I help you. This DNA business is critical. I hope you understand."

"If we took your memory away again, what do you think would happen to you?"

"You would have to be very selective. Suppose something went wrong and I didn't remember you at all. How would you convince me to do anything to help you? I might even be driven mad by your constant intrusion, not knowing where you came from, and be glad to be rid of you. Medical treatment could block you out, or otherwise render me useless to you. It's your risk."

Again there was silence, before they spoke next. "Very

well, we agree. You will have your chance. But once you have had it, you *will* help uss. What is it you want from us?'

"You have vast resources. Look for something that is so important it could slow up the discovery of DNA."

"It will be done."

"Are you all right?" Veema's voice.

"Yes. I'm OK."

"I thought I heard you talking to someone," she said.

"Did I wake you up?"

"Not really. I was only dozing. Was it the Asgathi again?"

"Yes, I'm afraid so. I may have to leave you again."

"I don't believe this word *may*. You're really going to leave me, aren't you?"

"Yes."

"This time, you might not come back. I'm not strong enough to do anything about rescuing you, this time."

"I know, but I must try to alter things. It's what my life's about."

"Where are you going, and what must you do?"

"I don't know. 0hhhh!" Moss felt overwhelming pressure in his head. X-rays, he thought.

"The discovery of X-rays led directly to the discovery of DNA. If a picture of the transverse section of the helix hadn't been taken, the discoverers might never have made the breakthrough," he said aloud. His voice sounded strange to him. Where did those words come from?

"The Asgathi are telling you to do something, aren't they?"

"I need to kill or discredit Wilhelm Roentgen." he said, dully.

Veema was desperate to stop him. "Think of all the good

things that x-rays have brought about," she said, "and the discovery of DNA wasn't all that bad. It just happened at the wrong time. You *must* listen to me, my darling. *Come back.*"

Moss was in the power of an irresistible force. He could hear Veema shouting for help, but it was all too late, much too late to turn back.

★ ★ ★

It was night. The cold crept through his coat and froze his un-gloved hands. Moss held a basket full of something that smelt familiar. When he lifted the cloth off the contents, he saw what looked like a loaf of bread. He looked up at a large building that loomed dark against a starlit sky. On the ground floor, a single window, covered by a thin blind, was lit by a lamp. The rest of the building was in darkness.

Where was he? *When* was he? *Who* was he?

Moss looked down at brown shoes tied with laces, trousers of a coarse brown weave, and a thick coat of similar material. It all felt very unfamiliar. He put his hand to his head. A hat? He felt further. A beard.

He knew instinctively that he must use the servants' entrance, which was at the back of the building. He passed an ornate metal archway over a gate. A path led up to an imposing front door. Attached to the arch, following the curve, were ornate letters that glinted dully in the feeble light of a nearby gas lamp. *Universität von Würzburg-Anstalt der Physik*. He was in the Bavarian town where Wilhelm Roentgen lived.

Moss found the servants' entrance without any trouble, as if he had been long accustomed to use it. The door creaked open. He had hardly stepped over the threshold, when he was greeted by a torrent of guttural speech from a large, plump woman wearing a dirty white cap, crimped round the edges. He knew what she was she was saying.

"Where the hell have you been? The Herr Doktor is waiting for his supper."

She snatched the basket from his grasp and put it down on a long, scrubbed kitchen table. The flames from half a dozen candles flickered in the draught from the door, and sent shadows dancing on the walls. There was a smell of cooked meat in the room that made Moss feel hungry. The woman held out a meaty hand, her fleshy lips curled back to reveal blackened teeth.

"The change, idiot!"

"What? Oh yes." He fumbled in a pocket and produced a handful of fluff, bits of string and a few coins.

"Ten *Pfennig* only? Where is the rest?"

"I don't know."

She made as if to cuff him round the ear, but he moved quickly out of range

"I don't know. What has got into you, Hans? Oh! for heaven's sake, do something useful. Cut up the Master's bread."

He started to pour water from a jug into a basin.

"What are you doing?"

"I am going to wash my hands."

"Whatever for? Get on with cutting up that bread."

"Yes, cook."

"And no more of your insolence."

Moss opened a drawer and pulled out a knife. It had a long, wide blade and a wooden handle, much scorched. With this, he started to try to cut the loaf into neat slices, but the knife was too blunt, and the bread ended up as crumbs.

"What is the matter with you today?" the cook said impatiently. "Come here. Give me the knife." She started to carve large chunks off the loaf.

He had to think fast, to explain his incompetence. "I have a headache. I may have a fever."

The cook backed off and looked at him. "Hmm," she grunted. She seized him by the arm, and pulled him up close to her. Her breath was rancid. "Open your mouth," she ordered, holding a candle to his face.

"Why?"

"*Open!*"

He obeyed. She examined the interior of his mouth.

"Show me your tongue. Huh! There doesn't seem to be anything much wrong with you." She placed her hand on his forehead. "No fever. You are just a lazy idiot."

She went to a cupboard and took out a small medicine bottle with a worn label. She took a teaspoon and poured out a spoonful of brown, sludgy liquid.

"Open your mouth."

Moss thought it would be unwise to disobey. He hoped it wouldn't be anything worse than a mild pain killer, or something equally innocuous. She tipped the liquid into Moss's mouth. It tasted vile.

The cook sighed. "I suppose you'd better clean the Herr Doktor's boots and go to bed. Make sure you're up tomorrow. You can finish what you should have done today."

He tried to keep the surprise out of his voice, and said, "Thank you, cook."

He spent the next fifteen minutes cleaning winter's mud of his master's boots and buffing them up to a good shine. When he had put away the blacking and brushes, he was ready for bed.

"Good night, cook."

"Goodnight, Hans."

He was halfway across the kitchen, when she shouted, "Haven't you forgotten something?"

Moss halted. Ye Gods, what was it now? He turned round and saw that she was holding out to him a candle in a candlestick, and a tinderbox.

"I told you I felt ill," he laughed feebly. "Thank you."

"Goodnight, Hans." She turned her back on him.

Leaving the warmth and comparative light of the kitchen, he went down the corridor and ascended the stairs. At the first landing, after a few unsuccessful attempts, he lit the candle. He was glad of its light; the higher he went, the darker it got. The gas lighting on the wall only extended as high as the first landing. After that, he had to climb slowly, with no more than the light of his flickering candle to show him the way.

Right at the top of the house, among the rafters, there was an attic room. A small, dirty window overlooked rooftops and the street far below. The attic obviously had a male occupant, judging from the trousers and other male attire untidily scattered about. There was a scratched chest of drawers. On its wooden top stood a jug, and a mirror with a crack in the bottom right hand corner. He set the candle down next to the mirror and looked at his reflection. His image stared back from it. It was not prepossessing. He saw lank brown hair, a bulbous nose, and full lips fringed with a short beard. A pair of blue eyes regarded him sullenly. In addition to the chest of drawers, the room boasted no other furniture, except for a narrow, rumpled bed.

He went to lie down on the bed, which creaked under his weight. He stared at the lath and plaster ceiling, trying to think what he was doing in this cold, dismal room, on this uncomfortable, damp bed. He had a job to do, and it was not to wait humbly on the cook or the Herr Doktor. He blew out the candle to conserve it.

He told himself that he must stay awake until the household had gone to bed. Then he would have to find out where, in time, he was. He had no idea of where in the house Roentgen's laboratory was to be found. Once he had located it, what was he going to do, when he got there? Smash up the Doktor's equipment and burn his notes? They could all probably be replaced. No, Moss thought, he would have to convince Roentgen not to continue with it his experiments. But how was he to do it?

With a start, he woke up. He hadn't meant to fall asleep. He hadn't realised how tired he was. Perhaps, that brown medicine had had something to do with it. Whatever time it was, he must get up now and get on with the job. He daren't risk falling asleep again. He went over and peered through the grimy window. It was still dark outside. That meant that he had to light his candle, and he was glad he had not let it burn away earlier.

He opened the door to his room, as quietly as possible, and crept down three flights of stairs to the ground floor. As he descended, he could hear the echoing tick of the hall clock. With a whir, as if the machine was gathering its breath, the clock chimed five times. It was later than Moss thought; perhaps, already too late.

Reaching the last stair, he looked about him. Before him was the front door. To his right was a heavy oak door. He moved quietly across the stone flags, opened this door, and found himself in a comfortable room. Pale light from the gas lamp in the street filtered through a gap in the heavy curtains. There were high-backed, upholstered chairs, and a large uncomfortable-looking sofa in the room. Next to one of the chairs was a small table, and on it was a newspaper. He picked it up and held his candle close to it. It was the edition of *Die Presse* dated the 27th December 1895. This, he knew, was the day before Roentgen's speech to the Physico-Medical Society, when he would reveal his research. So, today must be the 28th of December. He was already too late to stop this, unless he could do something about it right now.

He came out into the wide corridor. It was more like a hall, and it led off into the shadows. Trying to make as little noise as possible, Moss passed by some blackboards and charts on the walls. When he came to the end of the hall, a heavy oak door barred his way. He listened at it for a few moments, but could hear nothing. Then he tried the doorknob. It turned a bit, but the door wouldn't open. I'm a fool, Moss thought. Of course, Roentgen would lock it before he went to bed.

He bent down to the keyhole, but he could see nothing. That must mean that the door was locked from the inside. Roentgen must already be up and working, even at this hour. So much for an unobtrusive look at his laboratory!

Moss's heart began to beat furiously, and his mouth went dry. He needed to think of some pretext for getting inside the room. He would tell the professor that there was an urgent message from England. At five in the morning? It sounded unlikely, but it would have to do. He couldn't think of anything else. He would apologise, and tell Roentgen that went to bed last night with a headache and had forgotten to give his master the message.

Nervously, he banged on the door. Nothing. He knocked again.

"Herr Doktor, may I come in? It's Hans."

He heard heavy footsteps inside the room, and the door

was flung open. A tall, angry, bearded man stood before him, his long, dark hair standing straight up from his forehead. Piercing eyes looked down crossly at him.

"Yes? What is it, Hans? I'm busy," he said, in a full, deep voice. "Why aren't you at your duties?"

"I have a message for you, Herr Doktor, from England."

"From England? Ah! I am expecting one. Come in, Come in."

The room in which Moss found himself was small. It contained a large desk, and by the window there was a small table, covered with photographs. The walls were lined with shelves on which papers were piled untidily, and looked as if they were about to fall off. A door led off to a larger room, into which Roentgen had hurried.

"Come on! I'm very busy! Where is it?" The voice boomed.

Moss went through the door and found Roentgen bending low over a Crookes tube, on a laboratory bench.

"Read it out, man! I haven't got time to waste."

"I'm sorry, Herr Doktor, there is no message."

Roentgen looked as if he would explode with anger.

"What? Have you taken leave of your senses, idiot?"

Moss could think of nothing else but to launch straight into his explanation.

"I have to explain something to you, Herr Doktor, and it is very important indeed. Please, be patient and allow me a moment of your precious time. On the eighth of November, Herr Doktor, you were working with a Crookes tube; it was covered by a shield of a black cardboard. There was a strange glow on a screen, in the room behind you. The room was completely dark. It was night-time. You turned round and saw the screen glowing. You had made a wonderful discovery; something that will change the world."

Roentgen sat down heavily on a bench, and asked, "How can you know this?"

"This will be hard for you to accept, but I know because I am from the future."

For a moment, Roentgen looked shocked.

"This is a practical joke, yes?" he snarled, his cheeks red with anger. "Get out, you fool, and let me get on with my work."

"No, Herr Doktor, please listen. I'm perfectly serious."

Roentgen's fist came down on the lab table. "No! You are a spy! That is what you are!"

"I have come back in time, to warn you of the great danger the world is in, as a result of your work. You can't know this, but I do. It is far from being a joke. It is deadly serious."

"Nonsense. Who sent you? Becquerel? Yes. *I knew it!* Get out of here this instant! No. On second thoughts, stay here. I will send for the police."

Roentgen hurried from the room. He locked the outer door, and Moss heard his footsteps echoing down the corridor.

Moss had no alternative now. He must get away, and fast. He had no desire to end up in a Bavarian police cell. He looked around for an escape route. There was a large Georgian window, but when he tried it, he discovered that it was screwed shut. There was no other way out, and so Moss picked up a heavy stool and used it to smash a hole through glass and frame, in the bottom half of the window. He flung down the stool and squeezed through the hole. He dropped down into the garden next to the street, scrambled over the black iron railings and ran into the street.

★ ★ ★

The light was growing fast. He had to find somewhere to hide until the evening. He heard a clock chime eight o'clock. Nearby, church bells start to peal, calling the faithful to early mass. It was a normal working day, so far as Moss could judge. Stalls had already been set up in the square, vendors and housewives were busy, in spite of the early hour. The sharp cold of the December air made Moss realise that he was extremely hungry. He had eaten nothing. He had to have something to sustain him through the day. He felt in his pockets. In his left hand pocket he found a few copper coins. He separated them from the fluff. He hoped he had enough to buy something sustaining. He went to over to a stall and bought some bread and an apple.

"Out late this morning, aren't you, Hans? Isn't the Frau cook keeping you hard at it?" The stallholder laughed.

Damn! He'd been recognized.

"Yes. I just sneaked out. She's not very pleased with me, so I had no breakfast!"

"Ah, she's a tough one, that cook. You be careful now."

"I will."

He turned away and let the crowd swallow him up, out of sight of the stallholder. Moss didn't want the man to observe that he wasn't going back to the University. He entered an unfamiliar street; it curved and narrowed, its houses leant across the street. In places, their eaves extended so far that they almost touched the houses on the opposite side . He followed a pretty girl along an alleyway, and up a flight of steps. These gave onto a wide terrace on which was a tiny church, with scaffolding round it. Nearby, was an inn. He daren't go into it, in case he was recognized again. Already, Roentgen would have discovered the damage to his window, and the police would be out, looking for him. Perhaps the church would be the best place, if he could find a dark recess where he could hide himself. If he could, he should be all right.

He pushed open the heavy oak door, and found himself in a panelled porch with doors to his left and right. Yellowing notices were pinned to the wood. He closed the outer door carefully, and entered the nave by way of the left hand door. The air was thick with the smell of old polish and incense. There was no one about. Dust motes danced in the shafts of pale, winter sunlight beaming down from the windows. He found a side chapel; it had suitably a dark corner, where he felt safe to settle down with his bread and apple for breakfast, and endure a long wait. Dark red velvet curtains screened this sanctuary off from the nave. In spite of the cold, he fell into a doze.

He woke up with a shock, when he felt a light touch on his shoulder. An elderly priest was bending over him. Dusk had already fallen. The curtains had been drawn open, and a few candles, on the altar and before a shrine to Our Lady, provided fitful illumination.

"Are you all right, my son?"

"Yes, Father."

"Are you sure nothing is troubling you?"

"No, Father."

"The police came today, looking for someone. I told them nobody was here. If you are the man they are after, I would advise you to move out of town as soon as you can. It is dark outside. Where will you go? Do you have a bed for the night?" The priest eyed him gravely.

"I haven't done anything. I don't think the police can be

looking for me," Moss replied.

The priest sighed doubtfully, but said nothing.

"Can you tell me the time, please, Father?"

The priest fumbled in his robes and consulted a large pocket watch.

"It is seven o'clock."

"Then I must hurry. Can you tell me where the Physico-Medical Society meets? I'm a stranger to this town, come specially to hear the speaker tonight."

"The Physico-Medical Society. Mmmm. I'm not sure. Ah, yes, I remember now."

"Could you give me directions?"

"Of course. Even better than that: I will draw you a plan. Just wait a moment."

After the priest had been gone for a few minutes, Moss began to get very agitated. He heard a nearby clock strike a quarter past seven. Where had the old man got to? Then he heard slow, quiet steps approaching, and the priest returned.

"Sorry to be so long. Here you are. You see, this is the church, and this is the Institute."

"Thank you, Father."

"God go with you, my son. Excuse me now."

The priest trudged off into the darkness. Moss hoped he was not watching from behind a pillar. In any case, before he left the church, there was something Moss had to do. In the nave, in front of a thick pillar, on a pedestal, stood a statue of the Virgin Mary. The little candles on a small table in front of it had long since guttered out, but two larger ones still burned, one on either side of the statue. Steeling himself, he held his left palm over the flame. The smell and pain of his own flesh scorching nearly made him cry out. He had meant to submit his other hand to the same damage, but he couldn't bear the agony of it. One hand would have to sufficient.

Memorizing the plan, he thrust it into his pocket and set out for the Institute. It was very dark outside, the wind blew strongly. Only a few gas street lamps lit the way. Moss pulled his coat up round his ears, and walked quickly through the maze of streets.

A clock struck eight as he was approaching the Institute. There was no one at the door. He was late; he could hear the sound of voices and appreciative applause from within. Suppose it was already too late for him to carry out his plan?

He opened the street door, entered the foyer and ahead of him were double doors leading to the lecture theatre. To either side of the foyer, corridors led off, apparently to circle the theatre from the outside. He opened one door a crack, and saw that Doctor Roentgen was on his feet, every seat was occupied and people were even standing at the back. He certainly couldn't get in unobtrusively that way. At the rear of the room, between two people, he could see a door, which he guessed led out to the corridor. He hoped that he could get in through that door, without being noticed.

He followed the corridor, which was lit here and there by gas lamps, until he came to what he hoped was the right door. He opened just enough to give him a view of the theatre. He heard the sound of bodies shifting, and someone muttered an oath when he squeezed in.

Roentgen was in full flow. Moss waited for the moment when the Doktor was bending over some equipment, at which he moved along the gangway and sat down on one of the steps.

"It was with this apparatus that I created a photograph

of the bones in my wife's hand," Roentgen said, holding a blurry negative up to the light. While many of the audience gasped, most were unable to see the photograph clearly, but Roentgen's status was such, that few doubted the truth of his words.

Moss's stomach tightened, and he felt he could barely speak. If he were to act, it was now or never. If he let the Doctor go on to photograph the chairman's hand, thereby producing positive proof that he could do what he claimed he could do, all would be lost. He rose to his feet and stepped forward.

"It's a fake!" Moss's cried. His voice was more of a croak, but his words were clearly audible. A number of heads turned his way. He tried again, shouting louder this time. "It's a fake, I tell you!"

He saw Roentgen angrily scan the audience, looking for the man who dared to contradict him.

Now that he had everyone's attention, Moss walked further down the gangway. At the halfway point, he stopped; he dare go no further, yet. He turned and faced the audience, ignoring the Doktor.

"He wasn't getting anywhere with his experiments. He knew you were expecting to be shown something. He couldn't stand the disgrace of being called a fraud, and so he took the bones of a hand from a skeleton, outlined the fingers and thumb on a white card, cut out the shape and photographed both bones and drawing, superimposed on a black background, so the image looks like skin surrounding the bones."

Roentgen was convulsed with fury. "This is my servant, Hans, a man with very little brain. This morning, he actually told me that he was a man from the future. He is quite mad,

I tell you."

The crowd began to murmur, but all the faces remained riveted on Moss. For a moment, he let Roentgen seize the initiative.

"Look, I will prove this to you. Honoured chairman, I beg leave of you to help me that what I say is true. Would you kindly place your hand on this panel."

"Don't listen to him," Moss shouted. "He has already experimented on me. He forced me into a wooden box and shone his strange ray at my hand." Moss took his left hand out of his coat pocket and held it up, showing the burn on his palm to those seated nearest to him. A woman stood up, her hand to her mouth, and vomited.

The audience recoiled. The chairman stepped forward and appealed for calm. Then he turned to Roentgen again. "What have you to say about this, Herr Doktor? Is it true what this man says?"

"It is true that I have conducted experiments on living tissue."

"What about your wife? Why is she not here?" someone bawled.

Roentgen said quietly, "She is not well."

"What was that?" the heckler cried.

"I said that she is not well, but it is nothing whatsoever to do with my experiments."

"How do we know that?" another voice asked.

"Well, I for one will not be helping Herr Roentgen with his experiments, until I have proof of their safety," the Chairman said, desperate to quell what had all the makings of a riot. "Thank you for a most interesting evening, Herr Doktor. I'm sure we will be hearing more from you, but in the meantime, I would like draw these proceedings to a close."

The crowd began to disperse. Roentgen came off the dais and made his way towards Moss. His fists were clenched, and there was a look of cold fury on his face.

Moss couldn't move. A haze was coming between him and the advancing scientist. He felt himself collapsing. Then there was darkness.

– 14 –

Eye of the Storm

Moss heard his father's voice close by, but couldn't see anything in the gloom. He had not succeeded in changing the path that Roentgen was taking. He could hear his father explaining to him how, in the end, his servant Hans had confessed to being under the control of some evil entity.

"But, Moss, in spite of your failure, one man can make a difference. It's all about being in the right place at the right time. It is within your power to correct a case of potential bad luck. Without your intervention, the world will be a very different place."

"I don't understand."

"We know, because it has happened, but it's about to go wrong again. Someone iss polluting the time-liness. Britain could lose the war."

"Which war?"

"It was called The Second World War."

Moss heard a sickening roar and felt himself being tugged along, and squeezed through blackness. Feeling as if he had emerged from a tunnel at frightening speed, and come into the light, he opened his eyes to find himself looking up at a woman.

Mrs. Whittle was a heavily pregnant woman in her late twenties. She sat in a rocking-chair, beside a small fire that was burning quietly in a black leaded grate. Her four-year-old son Frank felt unwell. He had a chesty cough and a runny nose. He was looking at a book with a story in large print underneath the illustrations. He was lying on a rag rug. The clock on the mantelshelf struck seven. The woman put down her knitting.

"Your father will be home soon, Frank," she said. Do try and greet him properly this time. I'll just go and give the stew a stir."

She got up slowly and went out into the back kitchen. A coal settled and sent a shower of sparks flying up the chimney. Overhead, the gaslight whispered. The boy's eyes were tired and he was having difficulty in focusing on the rather uninteresting pictures of elves. He was much too old for elves, he thought. He wished his father would come home; maybe, after dinner, he would read something to him.

He heard the sound of footsteps, and his father's voice in the hall.

"Is that you, sweetheart?" Mrs. Whittle called from the kitchen.

"Who else would it be?" Frank's father spoke with a slight Midland's accent. The door into the sitting room opened, and a tall, thin man, aged about twenty-five, entered. He had a knapsack over one shoulder, and he set this on the floor, while he took off his overcoat, and Frank noticed that he was still dressed in blue overalls. His hair was brown and he wore a neat moustache. He grinned and held open his arms to the woman, as she came into the room.

"If you think I'm going to kiss you, while you're wearing those grubby things, you've got another thing coming," she said, smoothing her white apron over her swollen stomach. "Get those overalls off and have a wash. Supper's almost ready."

"And how've you been, young fella me lad, eh?"

The man stooped down and picked up Frank, as if he weighed nothing. The boy hated the feeling of being lifted into the air, and seeing the floor far below.

"I'm fine, father."

"I'm fine, Dad," the man mimicked, "and what sort of a greeting is that? Never mind, let's see what I've got you." He put Frank down. Both Moss and the boy were profoundly grateful.

The man fumbled in his knapsack and pulled out a tin aeroplane. The boy was thrilled. He smiled.

"Thank you, Dad. It's lovely."

"Give your father a kiss, then, Frank."

His father knelt down and put the small tin monoplane into the boy's chubby hand. Moss felt really strange about giving this man a slobbery kiss. The moustache smelt strongly of tobacco. He had to stop himself from recoiling in disgust. Young Frank was never very keen to kiss his father, either.

"What kind of 'plane is it, Dad?"

"It's one of those French jobs, a Bleriott, I think the man at the corner shop said it was. Have you got some thread, Mother?"

The woman went over to her sewing box and took from it a wooden reel of white twine. "This do?"

"Right enough. This is what we do with it. Give it here."

He took the 'plane out of the boy's hand and tied a

generous length of twine to a metal eye in the middle of the top surface of the wing, where it was attached to the fuselage. He cut off the surplus twine with a pair of dainty scissors from the workbox. Standing on a chair, he attached the free end of the twine to the ceiling gas bracket. Grasping the key sticking out of the side of the fuselage, which Moss hadn't noticed before, Frank's father wound up the clockwork and lowered the aeroplane on its twine. With a tinny whine, the aeroplane began to circle high above Frank's head. He looked up, entranced. The woman clapped her hands.

"What a wonderful present, isn't it, Frank?"

But the boy, with a huge grin on his face, continued to gaze up at the aeroplane, until the clockwork wound down.

"Make it go again, please," Frank asked, jumping up and down excitedly.

"Supper's ready," said the woman. "You can have another go afterwards. Give your father that post off the table, and help me lay up, will you dear?"

The boy obediently gave the letters to his father. Moss noticed that they were both addressed to Mr. Whittle. That name was familiar. Of course it was. The child Frank would someday invent the jet engine.

The scene in the small sitting room grew hazy and began to merge into another, like a dissolve in a film.

★ ★ ★

Frank was lying on his back on a bed. He could hear the sound of birdsong. Above him, a forest of model aeroplanes hung from the ceiling. There, in pride of place, directly overhead, was the clockwork model of Bleriot's early aircraft. There were also shiny aircraft, made of steel strips punched with holes, Meccano models, made by the boy. There were biplanes and monoplanes of all kinds. Through the open window he could see blue sky flecked with wisps of cloud.

"Frank! Frank!" His mother's voice floated up to him up from the kitchen.

He'd better reply. "Yes, Mother?"

"Your father will be here soon. Get your hands washed and help your sister to lay the table."

"Coming, Mother!"

He came downstairs slowly. The boy, now aged ten, just wanted to be quiet. It was good in Leamington Spa. He had countryside to roam and a garden to play in with his friends. He was glad that his father had made enough money as a foreman to buy a small business, and they had moved to a better place. The new baby had started crying, and his annoying younger sister was singing that awful song of hers. She wasn't interested in his aircraft, thank goodness. She thought they were silly.

He smelt the strong odour of cooked meat coming from the kitchen. Stew again, he grumbled, even though it was now high summer. He wished his mother would cook something else. They always had the same things for dinner, boiled meat and grey vegetables. This evening, it was the worst of meal of all: it was boiled beef and carrots, his father's favourite. The boy and Moss loathed the sight of it. Great lumps of fat clung to the meat in glutinous globs. He had, somehow, to choke it all down. Woe betide him, if he left anything.

The door opened and his father came in without a word. His sister stopped her incessant warbling. Even the baby went quiet. Mr. Whittle looked old and sad. His once brown moustache was now grey. Moss was appalled at the change in him. Surely, he couldn't have aged that much in the space of a mere five years or so. How old would the man be now? A particularly disgusting piece of fat made Frank gag, driving all other thoughts out of Moss's head. Mrs. Whittle gave him a thunderous look.

Then he heard the noise of an aero engine. It could only be coming from the back of the house. It certainly wasn't in the air. It was the sort of noise that bounced off the ground. The boy's heart lifted in excitement. Without thinking, he ate faster, forcing the fatty meat down. His mother looked even more annoyed. At last, he had cleaned his plate of every disgusting bit.

"Can I go out into the field?"

"No, you can't. We haven't finished here yet. There's Spotted Dick and custard for afters," she added by way of encouragement.

How could they eat this stodgy food? Moss thought. He could feel strong emotion welling inside the boy, whose thoughts broke through his own. Frank had never disobeyed his parents before, but this time was special. He might never have such a chance again. He wiped his greasy lips on his napkin, pulled back his chair and fled from the house.

He arrived at the gate at the end of the garden; he was feeling sick, his heart was pounding. The moment he saw it, however, he felt on top of the world. A Vickers Vimy was gleaming in the afternoon sunlight – the emblem of the Royal Flying Corps proudly displayed on the fuselage.

Frank ran out to meet it, waving and shouting, overwhelmed with happiness. But Moss was alert. The boy was too close to the propeller, too busy staring up at the cockpit. Moss heard the engine turn over. Something at the edge of memory, felt rather than heard, made him turn his head. Hurtling towards him was a man in a flat cap and tweed jacket, his face strangely blurred, so that Moss was unable to make out his features. Moss had the oddest feeling of being in two places at the same time, both in the man coming towards him and in the boy. The man was launching himself towards Moss, who ducked, and they fell in a heap together, just as the propeller blades roared overhead.

Moss expected to hit the ground hard. Instead, when he opened his eyes he was looking up at mist. He seemed to hang in nothingness. A voice spoke in his head, and he knew it was the voice of his father, who was saying, "On the fifteenth of May 1941, the Gloster E28/39 took off on its maiden flight. It already flew faster than the Spitfire. Very soon, it would fly faster still, and be the only aircraft able to shoot down Hitler's terror weapon: the V1 flying bomb. Meteors of 616 Squadron saved British cities from devastation, and Britain from what could have been a fatal loss of morale. Frank Whittle had so nearly died when the propellers of the Vickers Vimy started to turn, and had he done so, the Germans would have been the first to deploy a jet plane."

★ ★ ★

"You saved young Frank." The Asgathi spoke with the voice of Moss's father. "So, you can see how the life of one man was vital to history, as we told you. The death of one man can be equally vital. You can see how you helped your people. Now it is time for you to help usss.

"You helped me, so now I must help you?"

"Yesss."

"And to do this, you want me to commit murder?"

"Yesss."

"I won't do it."

"Do you think we can't reverse history?"

"Explain what you mean."

"You found yourself in two places at once, when you were inside the boy's mind?"

"What happened? I am so confused. I am forgetting who I really am."

"You had already been there, when the Vickers Vimy almost killed the boy. You hoped to avoid his death, by pushing him out of the way at the last moment. Instead, you knocked him under the wheels of the aeroplane, and he was crushed to death."

"I don't believe you," said Moss, horrified.

"Do you want uss to show you how it happened?"

Moss was appalled and incredulous. "No. No."

"It's such a trivial little thing. Von Stauffenberg didn't have such moral qualms about plotting to kill Hitler."

"But Hitler was a megalomaniac, truly evil. Who do want me to kill for you? I suppose that's what this is all about?"

"William Shockley."

"Who's he and why does he deserve to be killed?"

"Shockley was the co-inventor, with John Bardeen and Walter Brattain, of the semiconductor, which led to the microchip, which led to valve less computers, which ultimately led to spacecraft technology, and you remember how the Europa space probe will destroy uss."

"Why only Shockley? What will you do about Bardeen and Brattain?"

"They are not important. Brattain himself said Shockley was the catalyst who brought them together, and who suggested the idea that led to the breakthrough. Without him, and without the final despairing experiment made on Christmas Eve 1947, there would have been no semiconductor. All we ask you to do is to slow up the invention of the microchip, so as to give us more time to prepare ourselves to meet your Earth infections."

"And to do this, you want me to kill a perfectly good man?"

"Shockley wasn't a perfectly good man. His views became more and more extreme, similar to the ideas that led to the eugenics movement of the 1920s. That is the very thing you claim to be against. Shockley argued that the future of the population was threatened because people with low IQs had more children than those with high IQs. Can you honestly still call Shockley a perfectly good man, Mr. Moss?"

"But…"

"All right. Don't kill him. Let the Nazis take over Britain. We will leave you here, marooned, out of your body, and you will never see Veema again. You made us a promise. This is the price you must pay for breaking it. We Asgathi will find some other way of achieving our ends."

The image of his father was fading into the mist.

"Wait!" called Moss.

His father turned and asked, "What is it?"

"I apologise. What do you want me to do?"

"For once, you only have to step sideways in time. You see, Shockley was born in 1910, in London, to American parents. Frank Whittle was born in 1907, in Coventry. Breathe deeply and relax. We'll do the rest."

★ ★ ★

"I don't like this," Dalziel said.

Veema heaved herself off her bed and came over to him. "Doctors don't usually say things like that."

"I've got to be honest with you, Veema. Until now, all Moss's brain wave patterns were perfectly ordinary, nothing to worry about, despite your call for help. He was just deeply asleep and dreaming. Now, look at them; they're like they were when he was back in 1950."

"You mean to say the Asgathi have found a way to enable him to time travel without all the apparatus?"

"Not entirely. Once one pathway is established, it gets easier each time you want to establish another. I want you to try and touch the time jacket. Just trust me."

She put her hand out. A loud hum emanated from the jacket, when she was still thirty centimetres away. She pushed her hand further towards it. A pink aura, suffused with blue sparks, spread like a canopy over Moss. She felt a nasty tingling in her fingers.

"I wouldn't have let you do that if you hadn't been earthed to the floor. There's enough power in that jacket to throw you across the room."

"How long have you known about that?"

Dalziel looked worried. "After you called, I came in and checked on him, and he was fine. This has only happened in the last minute or so. It was when I went to touch him, to check his temperature, the same thing happened to me."

"I didn't notice that," she said, wrinkling her brow. "I can't have been watching you. What happens next?"

"I don't know," Dalziel said, "but it doesn't look good."

– 15 –

The Storm Breaks

The first thing that assaulted Moss was noise: a whining, sucking, clunking sound that was getting on his nerves. He opened his eyes and found he was sitting, looking at a white-painted, panelled door. Involuntarily, as if under the control of someone else, he got up. He wondered whose mind he was sharing this time. Something slid off his knees. He looked down. Her knees. It was a woman. She was wearing an old-fashioned, long, white apron, covering a grey skirt and white blouse. A newspaper lay on the floor in front of her. She stretched out a veined hand to open the door. Breathing seemed to be quite difficult, constricted. Moss was about to discover who she was.

"Alice, do you have to make such a din?" The voice was not aristocratic but it was cultured and authoritative.

The maid, Alice, glanced up from the half landing, a stray black curl escaping from her white cap. She looked hot and flushed; there was sweat on her forehead.

"Can't 'elp it, nanny. It's this newfangled machine what 'er ladyship bought. She's told me to give the 'ole 'ouse a good goin' over with it, while they're away on business. It ain't 'alf 'eavy, I can tell yer. Give me a brush'n pan, any day."

"That's as may be, but you'll wake Master William with that racket."

"Nearly finished."

Nanny closed the nursery door and leant against it. It had been so much quieter, when she was young. Now, there were all sorts of things to disturb the household: gramophones, refrigerators, washing machines. In fact, there were all manner of electrical gadgets; all making so much noise that life was becoming intolerable. One used to be able to come in, shut the door and relax. Now, there was noise on the inside, as well as on the outside. She disliked this new electricity and found it rather tiring to the eyes. Gaslight was gentler.

Moss had difficulty in tuning out all Nanny's thoughts about this trivia. This warned him that he was obviously in the grip of a very strong character. He looked around what was had to be the nursery. Sunshine streamed through the net curtains, glanced off the pink-distempered walls, and brightened up the rather dull carpet, with its formal pattern of trees and roses. There was a small fire in the black-leaded grate; this and the sunshine indicated that it was probably early spring.

The baby lay asleep in its cradle, the holes in the wicker weave patterning the coverlet with sun and shadow.

Moss looked at the baby, so innocent and peaceful, and asked himself how he could possibly kill it. Suppose he were looking at the infant Stalin, or Pol Pot. If he had known their identity, would it have been easier?

Nanny walked over to the baby, and Moss felt her thoughts superimpose themselves on his.

"What a noisy old world you've been born into, Master William."

Mr. and Mrs. Shockley, William's parents, were well able to provide for him. Mr. Shockley was a mining engineer, and his wife was employed as a deputy surveyor. Moss was remembering his mission and the background to the prospective victim's family.

Nanny was thinking that mothers of young children didn't go out to work, when she was young. The Shockleys had plenty of luxuries; when she was growing up, her parents had barely enough to feed her and her siblings.

Moss looked down at the cradle, while nanny's thoughts were busy raking over the past. It would be too obvious if the baby were to be found dead here, in the house. Nanny would be the only suspect. What did he care? He would be well out of it, or would he? Would the Asgathi deliver on their promise, or just leave him here, to rot, once they got what they wanted? They had now shown themselves to be unfeeling, interested only in their own self-preservation. But, he thought, wouldn't he be behaving like them, if he were in their situation?

Nanny went back to her chair and picked up her newspaper. She began to read an article about a new, up-and-coming Parliamentary party that claimed to represent working-class people.

"I'm in favour of these people," she said softly. "It's a pity, though, that I can't vote for them. I wonder if we women will ever get the vote."

Moss looked at the date on the top of the newspaper: April 10th, 1911.

Somewhere in the depths of the house, a clock chimed ten o'clock. Nanny looked down at the watch hanging upside down from her white apron. "Time for baby's feed."

The maid was industriously brushing the stairs. Nanny heard her, and got up to open the door. The smell of beeswax was heavy in the air. Alice was just finishing the last bit of stair carpet outside the nursery door.

"It's ten o'clock, Alice."

"I know, Nanny," said the maid, wearily.

"See if cook's got baby's milk ready. It's time for his feed."

The maid looked past Nanny into the nursery, and protested, "But, he's asleep!"

"Less of your lip, my girl. Baby's routine works with precision."

"You're worse than 'er ladyship," said Alice.

Moss could feel impatience boiling up inside Nanny. Her thin lips creased into a line, and her formidable jaw jutted out above her lace collar.

"Yes, Nanny." Alice sighed, put down the dustpan and brush, and began to make her way down the creaking stairs.

"And, Alice, don't leave the dustpan where someone might trip over it!"

The maid winced. "No, Nanny."

She came slowly back up again and retrieved the dark green brush and tray.

Nanny waited until the girl reached the bottom of the stairs, and then swept back into her domain and waited until Alice returned with the white china feeding bottle with a pattern of blue trees on it. Later, after William had been fed and burped, she put him back in his cradle, and resumed her study of her newspaper. She found it soothing to rock back and forth in her rocking chair by the fire.

Moss found that, as long as he didn't try to influence her behaviour, things carried on as normal. While her mind was distracted by unimportant things, he could think about what he was going to do. Having held the child, and looked into its eyes, he knew he couldn't do it any harm. It was one thing to kill someone you didn't know, hadn't seen before, in an instant, but it was altogether different now. Another difficulty

– in fact, more than just a difficulty – was the fundamental question: was this really happening? It could be an illusion, created by the Asgathi to test him. The whole Frank Whittle incident could have been a way of manipulating him into agreeing to their plans. He might have changed history, and changed it again, or it could all have been elaborate trickery. The more he thought in this way, the more it bothered him.

He decided to try an experiment. He imagined that Nanny's nose was very itchy. She wanted to scratch it. She *really* wanted to scratch it. Yes, yes, one hand was coming up. Her index finger scratched her nose. She resumed her newspaper.

Well, that was real enough. Or, perhaps the Asgathi had created the *illusion* that she felt the need to scratch. It was all getting alarmingly confusing. Moss felt that, for now, the best thing would be, to assume that what was happening now was, indeed, happening – and Nanny scratching her nose had proved that he had been able to influence her actions, albeit in a tiny way, just then. He was also prepared to assume that he was in 1911, and that the Asgathi had no ability to influence him, at this distance in time. But, he had to do something about young William, otherwise the Asgathi would carry out their threat, and he would never be able to do what he had set out to do for humankind: improve the society in which he was living.

Something in the paper caught nanny's eye. Under a large headline, 'Horrible Accident', was a report that said: 'Mr. and Mrs. Blenkinsop were mourning the loss of their son, Arthur, who died in a serious automobile accident, in Peckham yesterday.' The article related how the one-year-old child had been run over and crushed in his pram, while Mrs. Blenkinsopp was on her way home after visiting friends. A car had come round a bend and smashed into them. Drunkenness on the part of the driver was suspected. Mrs. Blenkinsop was unhurt, but in a state of shock. The Blenkinsops had only one other child, called John, who was seriously ill with pneumonia in King's College Hospital. It gave their address, which nanny recognised as being in a lower middle-class area. The mother had been a Post Office clerk and the father worked as a postman.

Moss knew instantly what he should do, but Nanny's schedule must not be disrupted. If the nursery routine did not to proceed as usual, it would be remarked upon in the household. It was time for William's walk. While Nanny was occupied with that, it would give Moss time to think.

It was clear that Nanny loved showing off the baby, in his shiny, black perambulator with the fringed hood. She could pretend, for a little while, that William was all hers.

Despite being such a formidable character, her love for the child was her Achilles' heel. She carefully descended the stairs, tenderly holding her charge. The baby was swathed warmly against the spring chill; only his pink face was showing. She was proud of him for being such a well-behaved child. He burbled quietly, while she spoke to him in a sweet, low voice that quite belied her forbidding exterior.

In the yard at the back of the house, the gleaming black perambulator stood ready. Its chrome work glittered in the sunshine. Placing William carefully inside and pulling the covers up round him, she pushed the perambulator triumphantly past the open doors of the garage. A man in a striped, collarless shirt, braces holding up his trousers, was hard at work, polishing an impressive Rolls Royce motor car.

"Good Morning, Hudson," she greeted the chauffeur.

"Good Morning, Nanny. Nice day for a walk. How's the

young monster?"

Nanny didn't deign to reply, but pushed the perambulator, clattering and crunching, over the cobbles of the yard and out into the noisy street. An omnibus went by, its horn blaring, sending people scattering out of its way. People were jostling one another on the crowded, narrow pavement, and not one of them stopped to look at her little treasure. She felt affronted.

Moss had been thinking about the hospital where John Blenkisop was a patient, and his thoughts had somehow leaked across into Nanny's subconscious. In her younger days, she had been a hospital nurse and had worked in the same hospital.

She was reminiscing about it. King'sCollege Hospital was in Denmark Hill, not far from the Shockley's house. Nanny thought she'd like to revisit the place. It was no distance, and so she walked there and parked the perambulator outside a small service entrance. She took out the gently cooing William and, carefully wrapping him up, she made her way through a maze of familiar corridors, until she came to the children's ward. There were no nurses to be seen, and the sound of chatter came loudly from the tearoom. She passed quietly by its open door and entered the ward.

Pale watery sun shone through the tall windows and illuminated long rows of cots, which stretched in serried ranks along both walls. The strong smell of Lysol disinfectant made her nose twitch and she had to work hard not to sneeze and draw attention to herself.

She looked closely at the names on the ends of the cots. She came to one cot that bore a label with the name John Blenkinsopp. Over the bed hung a green canopy, like a tent suspended on guy ropes. Nanny peered inside. Two containers, one at the head and one at the foot of the cot, filled the air under the canopy with an antiseptic mist. Despite this, the small patient did not seem to be breathing. Nanny put William down carefully on the floor, and put her ear close to the child's face. He was dead.

This was more than Moss had hoped for. He used every ounce of concentration in order to get control of nanny's actions. He knew that she would instinctively resist him.

Picking up the lifeless child, she exchanged him for William, whom she tucked up in the cot, so that only his face showed.

It was becoming more and more difficult for Moss to stop Nanny's thoughts from hindering him, but he had to succeed.

Lifting the dead baby from the floor, she hurried to the end of the ward, out of the service doors, and down a maze of back stairs. When she arrived back at the street door service entrance, she was breathing heavily.

She leant against the wall for a moment, clutching the dead child to her bosom.

Moss shared the misery she felt over the loss of a young life, but this misery was threatening to overwhelm him. He could not let that happen; if he did, he would lose control and all this would have been for nothing. So far, it had worked beyond his wildest dreams. He only hoped that the Blenkisops would be taken in by William, and accept him as their one remaining child. They would be so desperate to believe he was theirs, Moss hoped, that they would not be suspicious. The boys were both so tiny, after all, and, as far as Moss knew, were difficult to recognise, even for doting parents. They looked remarkably similar. The parents would be thrilled at their baby's miraculous recovery. They would give thanks to God that their prayers, and those of the church to which they belonged, had been answered.

Nanny placed the dead child in the perambulator, and slowly wheeled it out of the side street and back into the noise and smell of Denmark Hill.

Now Moss needed to arrange the same fate for John Blenkinsop as the Asgathi had willed for William Shockley. The tiny body would have to be rendered unrecognizable, even though the Shockleys would demand the inevitable investigation. Nanny wheeled the perambulator down the hill, to the crossing, where she stood irresolute. Moss managed to wipe from her mind all memories of what had just transpired. She was taking little William home.

The busy main road was heavily mired, and she involuntarily stood back from the carriageway, to avoid her clothes being splashed.

"Sweep the crossing for you, Miss? Only a penny."

Nanny was taken by surprise by the small, smelly urchin, who was looking up at her, his grubby hand extended. Nanny looked down at him from a great height. Normally, she wouldn't give such a child a second glance. For some reason, her reaction today was somehow different from usual. She let go of the handle of the perambulator and fumbled in her bag for her purse.

Moss knew that it was now or never. Could he pull off what he'd done with Eva Moss, back in Sutton Park? He concentrated with all his might.

"Nanny," he warned, forcing her subconscious to respond, "there's a glob of something forming in the back of your throat. It won't go away. You've got to cough it up."

Nanny coughed genteelly. The obstruction remained. She took out a lace handkerchief and coughed discreetly into it. The glob still restricted her throat.

Moss strained his hardest, to keep her distracted from the perambulator for a few moments more.

The perambulator was beginning to move down hill, skewing to the left, but not fast enough for Moss. He had seen a black car pull out from the side of the road. Timing was everything, at this stage.

Nanny closed her eyes, overtaken by a paroxysm of coughing. She bent double, turned and slid on the mud underfoot. She fell sideways against the perambulator, which rolled off the pavement and into the path of the car. The driver hooted, panic-stricken and unable to brake in time. Too late, she realised what was happening and tried to rush after the perambulator. The baby carriage disappeared, with an audible crunch, under the wheels of the car.

"My baby! My baby!" she screamed, her throat constricted, tears streaming down her cheeks. Some passers by stopped to offer help, or to get a closer look. The pram had been smashed to pieces by the impact, and the front axle of the car had come to rest where the baby's head would have been.

Nanny was dimly aware of a police constable pushing his way towards her.

"You all right, madam?" he asked.

Unable to reply, Nanny fainted in his arms.

Moss tried to call out, but Nanny's mind was enclosed in darkness.

Veema was worried. Moss had been away far too long. Suddenly, in horror, she saw that his brain trace was flattening out. She reached for the emergency button, to summon Dalziel, and everything went black.

– 16 –

Rendezvous

Veema woke up, or rather, she jerked awake, as if and she'd been given an electric shock. It was most unpleasant. The room was dark. She turned on her side, put on the bedside light, and looked at the old-style alarm clock. It was three in the morning; the time when people are most often at their lowest ebb; the time when some unhappy people finally give up and die.

Already, her dream was fading. It had been the most real, most vivid dream she'd ever had. She had been on a rally, protesting against the eugenics policy of the government. She had been holding up a banner proclaiming: NATURAL SELECTION – NATURAL BIRTH. "The Blenkinsop Law", as everyone called it, was creating more and more unrest amongst the population. She believed passionately that every foetus had a right to life, whatever the lineage or status of its parents.

She'd seen a man on the BBC. He'd become the idol of her life. Nobody knew what his real name was. People called him Loratu. In her dream, she had met him, fallen love with him and he with her. However, today, she would have to face harsh reality. She'd had the summons in the post. This was the day when the man from the Department of Sterilization was coming to see her. She'd already packed a suitcase, for her visit to the hospital, but she still wasn't sure whether she would submit to being sterilised, or whether she would try to disappear. She didn't want to leave her comfortable flat and the life she knew, but she had to choose one thing, or the other.

She switched off the light and lay back on her bed. There were only a few hours to go before the man was due to call.

By seven, she was up, dressed and breakfasted. The buzzer on the front door sounded. This was the moment she'd been dreading. She went out into the small, dark hall and looked through the spy hole in the front door. The lens showed a man a grey suit; he was wearing sunglasses and carrying a black briefcase.

She opened the door as wide as the short safety chain permitted. It snapped taut. The morning light and the sound of traffic flooded in.

"What do you want?" she said, squinting through the gap.

The man held out an open, black wallet, revealing his identity card.

"Veema Price?"

"Who wants her?"

"Sterilization. We have an appointment."

"Yes, of course you do. Is there any reason why I should let you in?"

"It's the law. You know what happens to women with insanity in the family. Our records show that your maternal grandmother spent some time in an asylum for the insane. I'm only doing my job. I didn't make the law, miss."

"You've only come to talk to me. Right?"

"Yes, that's correct."

"But I'll never be allowed to have children, and that's unfair. I'm perfectly sane. I work as a nurse. Do you think I wouldn't know it, if there were something wrong with me?"

"You know the law. An abnormality has been found in your family. It's a risk the state can't afford to take, nurse, or not. I'm sorry, but that's the way it is."

These words crystallized her thoughts. No, it's a risk *I* can't afford to take, she told herself.

She threw herself hard against the door, and managed to close it just as he was putting his foot into the crack. She ran into the kitchen, grabbed the small suitcase she'd packed for the hospital, and was out of the back door and running down the road, even as she heard the front door splinter.

The Underground station was not far away, and she was soon lost in the crowd hurrying to work. As she about to descend the escalator, she saw a policeman and thought that he was scrutinising her too closely. She panicked and rushed down onto the platform. Bruised and shaken, she boarded the packed train just as the doors were about to close. She found a handhold and clung to it as the train swayed through the darkness of the tunnel. Thankfully, she realised that the commuters in her carriage were studiously avoiding eye-contact with one another, and she felt able to relax.

Somewhere, he was out there. She had to find him. Her Loratu would know what to do.

* * *

Moss woke up. Someone was bending over him; a strikingly handsome woman with a pale faces and grey eyes. Dark blue veins showed under the thin skin of her forehead.

"Camille! What are you doing here?"

She looked at him strangely. "I'm your wife. Why shouldn't I be here?"

"My wife," he said faintly. He looked around the bare,

whitewashed room. He felt light-headed. The Asgathi had gone. That must mean…

"Where are the others?" Moss asked.

"What others?"

"Veema, Bartok, Elnac, Dalziel."

With each name he mentioned, she looked more and more perplexed.

"What are you talking about? Who's this Veema?" she asked suspiciously.

"They were here, just a moment ago. Tell me something. What year is this?"

"2050. What's the matter? Surely you know what year it is."

"2050. Right. Where's the computer? I must access the Internet."

"The Internet? What are you babbling about?"

With each answer Camille gave, Moss became more and more sure that he had succeeded, and given the Asgathi what they wanted. He would ask Camille one more question. If she replied, "no," he would know it for certain. If baby William Shockley had not grown up to discover the point-contact transistor, there would be no computers and, therefore, no space travel.

"Has man landed on the moon?"

"What a stupid question, of course not. How would he get there? Lie back. I don't think you're at all well."

She pushed him back and patted his pillow reassuringly.

"Look, I know what'll cheer you up. You're going to be a father soon. The Blenkinsop Commission has passed me fit for motherhood. I'm in the clear. No genetic hang ups in my family. Isn't it a good thing that you chose to marry me?"

For a full list of Lolfa publications,
send now for our new, free, full-colour
Catalogue – or why not surf into our
website

www.ylolfa.com

where you may order books on-line.